LORENZO THE MAGNIFICENT

ALSO BY ROBERT FRANKLIN LESLIE

Robert Franklin Leslie

DRAWINGS BY

PATTI ANN HARRIS

New York London

LORENZO

the Magnificent

THE STORY OF AN

ORPHANED BLUE JAY

W·W·NORTON & COMPANY

639.978
L

Published simultaneously in Canada by Penguin
Books Canada Ltd. 2801 John Street, Markham,
Ontario L3R 1B4
Printed in the United States of America.

The text of this book is composed in Bembo, with display type set in
Bernhard Modern. Composition and manufacturing by The Haddon
Craftsmen, Inc. Book design by Margaret M. Wagner.

First Edition

Library of Congress Cataloging in Publication Data
Leslie, Robert Franklin.
Lorenzo the Magnificent.
1. Blue jay. 2. Wildlife rescue. I. Title.
QL795.B57L45   1985   639.9'78864   84–20719

ISBN 0-393-01974-8

W.W. Norton & Company, Inc.
500 Fifth Avenue, New York, N. Y. 10110
W.W. Norton & Company Ltd.
37 Great Russell Street, London WC1B 3NU
1 2 3 4 5 6 7 8 9 0

For
my wife
LEA ROCHAT LESLIE
with deepest love
and understanding

Villon among the birds is he.
A bold bright rover, bad and free;
Yet not without such loveliness
As makes the curse upon him less.
                              —Louise Driscoll

LORENZO THE MAGNIFICENT

1

IT WAS A NOISY EVENING IN MARCH because a Santa Ana wind was howling across Southern California's San Fernando Valley. My good friends, Helen Addison Howard and her husband, Ben, were being walked by their dog alongside the Walt Disney Studios in Burbank. As the couple stepped to the street, a tinny voice squeaked from the gutter. The big German shepherd, instantly alerted, pointed out a golf-ball-sized puff of dark gray down lying in muddy debris. A short time later my telephone rang.

"Bob, we've just picked up a wounded baby blue

jay," Helen said. "We're on our way to your place."

Wild orphans—four-legged, two-legged, and no-legged—have somehow found their way to my tent, wickiup, apartment, cabin, farmhouse, or sleeping bag ever since I was a country boy on Leon River bottom-land in west Texas. My Victorian mother, somewhat prejudiced against several forms of wildlife, often threatened to approach my sleeping quarters with a shotgun. So it was not altogether unreasonable for my friends, Ben and Helen, to make what might otherwise have sounded like a nervy announcement. People were always delivering little waifs.

The jaychick arrived—shaggy, seriously wounded, clubfooted, filthy, and probably in shock. A broken leg and wing were minor concerns compared with the wound on top of its head. Some hostile creature had peeled his scalp to the bone. His beak had suffered such a twist that both mandibles were crossed like your fingers when you tell a whopper. When the moving membrane between his eyelids and eyeballs failed to open and close, I was afraid he had also suffered lethal brain damage.

Over many years in our secluded nook of the San Fernando Valley, my wife Lea and I operated a kind of burweed orphanage-clinic for wildlings. Because of assorted and often exotic noises that our clinic fre-quently emitted, nearby harassed neighbors sometimes referred to it as "the Loonybin." Bedrooms, living room, den, service porch, kitchen, garage, backyard cages—even a small treehouse—at one time or another (depending upon current inpatient or outpatient species) served as hospital for the sick and wounded or as youth hostel for tired, lost, or wayward wildlife. But of all the ragpicked specimens ever to reach our "Emergency Door," this infant jay looked like our most hopeless case. Giving the pitiful creature only a few hours to live, I didn't even bother to write up a sick chart. Still, we considered it our duty to tranquilize the little fellow with a few drops of sodium pentobarbital, then patch his torn, twisted, and broken body as best we could.

The decision afforded little certainty of success. The more I looked at the anesthetized jay the more hopeless he seemed . . . and the more miserable he made me feel. Before the roily night was out, I was sorely tempted in the name of mercy to use the hatchet, but Lea and I are soundly convinced that we were not created to be executioners of wounded wildlife. And so we cleaned and patched until 5:00 A.M.

Finding the baby jay still alive at midmorning, we looked for a glimmer of hope in that little padded box full of disaster. With eyes that somehow sparkled— as only a blue jay's can—the grubby urchin tottered on his clubbed foot, fluttered his unbroken wing, shrieked like a milermore bird (which can be heard for a *mile or more*), and looked from one of us to the other. The little guy was demanding food and water!

Lea rushed to blend pet-store vitamins, a hard-boiled egg, Cream of Wheat, milk, honey, peanut butter, and a pulverized carrot: F.F.F.F. (otherwise known around the neighborhood as Lea's Formula for the Fortification of Fledgling Fowl). With a tooth-pick and an eyedropper we stuffed and pumped food and water down that eager throat. The bird was barely beyond the helpless stage in his development. His breast was naked of down; thus a stuffed craw contributed to the look of full-blown catastrophe in miniature.

Immediately upon admitting new inpatients to the clinic, we generally began a chart, then—like the doctor who disappears into his inner sanctum in order to read up on his new patient's ailment—dashed off to the public library to research specific needs of the species in the "waiting room." Seed-crackers and meat-eaters in our care posed no greater problem than the money it took to buy their groceries. But what in the world do you feed an infant jaychick? Our local branch of the Los Angeles Public Library offered the most meager definition of a blue jay, let alone any information on the species; so we hurried to the main affiliate in Los Angeles, reputedly one of the outstand-

ing reference sources on birds in the nation. Endless cross-reading, cross-references, one crossed-up computer, and a cross-eyed attendant yielded little reliable information on jaybird diet.

At length we took the advice of friends and ran an ad in the *Valley Times:* "Wanted, information on the feeding and care of an orphan blue jay."

Meanwhile, our little patient clung to life with F.F.F.F. and exercised a noisy disposition, if not growing muscles. How were we to know that jaychicks ate every half hour? Somebody called in that information after reading our ad.

So, forty-eight times a day, with the aid of a bell timer, we crammed Lea's gooey mixture down the jay's cooperative throat and washed it into his crop with distilled water and goat's milk (another call-in).

We had discovered years before that water from city pipes gave little birds the colic—and worse (we've seen the insides of city pipes). Hence, we always used distilled water.

No matter how stormy these feeding encounters were, nothing capsized that jay's appetite. Between stuffings, our patient, unable to perch with splinted wing and leg, bandaged head, crossed beak, and clubbed foot, wobbled on his knees into one corner of an assigned holding cage and dozed on shredded newspaper. We kept the cage in the family den where the temperature remained constant at 68° F.

Still insecure about baby blue jay diet, we returned to the L.A. Central Library. One dedicated librarian rolled a cartload of literature into the reading room: volumes of crazy, outdated abstracts that should have been filed long before in the Department of Useless Information. For example, "The entire jay family symbolizes contention, discord, and strife," said one article. Another "authority" stated with startling mastery of his subject the following pearl: "Wild jays fly from crib to crib of other species, jabbing their beaks against the crops of nestlings, forcing them to puke up the food that parents had just fed them. Adult jays either race home to their own offspring with the up-chuck or wolf it themselves on the spot!" The exclamation point is mine.

Another article asserted that jays enjoyed a varied

diet, including raw worms (whoever heard of a *cooked* worm!), insects, fruits, nuts, acorns, and other birds' eggs, "but they prefer the bulk of their food filched from scarce pickings." Whatever that meant.

After dozens of hours, we simply used our own judgment in light of the fact that birding has been a year-round activity with Lea and me for more years than we care to admit.

During the course of that long experience, most of our foundlings and doorstep castaways have perked up, ready—after several weeks of Lea's Formula—to tangle with the outside world. Whenever a fledgling convinced us that he or she was on the mend, we added soaked raisin bits to the basic Formula, along with fruit juices, chopped sunflower kernels, wheat germ, suet, ground acorns, and bone meal—depending, of course, on the species at hand.

After two weeks of notable improvement, we reduced our jay's feedings to three hefty meals a day and no food after 6:00 P.M. To be sure, he was not a hummingbird, most of which required feeding at thirty-minute intervals during daylight hours. Raptors, such as an orphan screech owl we raised and called Olie, had seemed to thrive on much less than the jay.

With gluttonous gusto the jaychick gulped every morsel we shoved down his throat. He even tried to swallow the eyedropper from which we pumped an endless flow of fortified milk, fortified juices, fortified consommés, and *unfortified* water. The final price of having advertised for information about jaybird diet was a losing battle with local "experts" over the daily quotas of proteins, carbohydrates, and polyunsaturated everythings. Southern Californians are fiercely proud of their stewardship record with feathered wildlings. With the best of intentions, do-gooders in this category from far and near brought frightening quantities of what they declared was "typical jaybird fare." Opposing factions assured us that the little jay was about to eat his way into monsterhood. We received donations of popcorn soaked in doe's milk . . . and sticky taffy that was supposed to keep him pacified and at the same time untwist his twisted beak! So, we had the only bird with a sweet *tooth!* One member of the local Audubon Auxiliary spent a weekend gathering and grinding ripe acorns. Our bird, she avowed, was a scrub-oak jay—not a crested jay—and *must* have a daily quota of acorn meal. When I asked the dear soul where mother jays got acorns ground into meal for their nestlings, she scowled and ignored my impertinence. A couple of jay fanatics sent a case of earthworms and a pound of mealworms, delivered to our door by a local fish bait dealer. Guess who paid the bill!

In noisy blue jay tradition, our fledgling gobbled

the F.F.F.F. and everything else, then yelled for more. When mealworms were no longer forthcoming, he became about as congenial as an albatross.

Most of the anecdotes in the story that follows here are somewhat unconnected—simply told "as is" from a notebook we kept on the rambunctious bird. The account is, however, sequential so far as happenings are concerned. Our aim is not to prove scientific premises but to entertain . . . to share our ups and down-and-outs with one ornery but lovable jay as he grew to take over our household. Although the story is true in every detail, perhaps we have taken certain liberties in our *interpretations* of specific uninhibited behavior. You be the judge. You may come up with better explanations if you decide to foster-parent a blue jay.

One bit of jay science, then we shall proceed. Jays belong to a bird family called the *Corvidae*. That means they are part of the raven bunch, which may explain the word *ravenous* as applied to our patient's formidable appetite.

To save time and effort, we experimented with several automatic feeding devices designed to deliver maxi-bites to the hungry jay every time he tapped a trigger mechanism with his crooked beak. We soon learned, however, that automatic feeding tubes became clogged unless they dispensed dry food or runny liquids. Our formula was gooey, and our bird was too screwy to learn to operate an automatic feeder. My own inventive talent was limited to a left-handed corkscrew, which was a failure because the corks always ended up inside the bottles.

On one rash spending spree, I invested in a small cake decorator—the canvas kind with a metal nozzle that bakers use when they concoct fancy icings. With this gizmo we could squeeze F.F.F.F. down the jaychick's throat as he crouched either in his cage or on the kitchen counter, mandibles spread wide and legs coordinated to receive all contributions. In the end the gadget was a dismal failure . . . not from the jay's viewpoint. From ours. The fabric cornucopia, forgotten one night, set and dried into a cementlike monolith. Nonbiodegradable, nonreclaimable.

We didn't want to think about what would have happened if that formula had set up in the jay's pipes. . . .

Deciding that there was no honestly easy or economical way to gorge the growing bird, I whittled a small hardwood ladle that held exactly the right size jaybites. The little fellow hung onto that ladle like a fifth-grader who chews for extra mileage on an all-day sucker stick.

Besides feeding information, we learned jaybird facts piecemeal, here and there. As you may have known for years, jays hatch naked, and their eyes don't open until they are nine days old. Everyone seemed to know that but us. Without constant parental hovering, jaychicks cannot retain body heat for their first two weeks of life. Our baby jay must have been about three weeks old when he fell—or was shoved—from the family cradle, because tiny buds of primary and secondary pinions had begun to sprout. In fact, nothing more definite than his long, ebony-scaled legs and a devilish scowl identified him as a blue jay when he first came to us, except that Ben and Helen had so classified him. At the base of his beak, half-inch-long black whiskers gave his face the half-finished look of a clown. The effect was about as flattering as a mustache on a homecoming queen.

Our little jay's bloated exhaust pipe worked overtime. It appeared likely that his parents had fed him poisoned bugs before he plunged from the nest. It was even probable that the poison still purged him. We knew that trees in the Burbank neighborhood had been sprayed with chlordane and lindane, so it was no fault of the bird's parents that he was half-dead with diarrhea. In the nick of time Lea added kaopectate and paregoric to the F.F.F.F. For each evacuation thereafter, the jaychick hobbled across the cage floor, turned around, and guanoed his outside world, namely, one wall of the den. Blue jays tolerate no long periods of toilet training *inside* the family bassinet (I read that bit of esoterica somewhere).

During those first uncertain days our bird learned to call incessantly, making no attempt to conceal his dislike for caged solitude; yet when we approached without food, he bounded against the wire bars as if bent on freedom or self-destruction. Considering long experience with other wild birds, our ignorance of jays was impressive. We thought his grim determination to escape would diminish the more we left him to his own devices. The opposite is true of jays. They'd rather cuddle with cats than be left alone.

By remaining close to him, at last we earned his confidence and shaky peaceful coexistence. You don't demand a bird's respect; you earn it. We began carrying the cage from room to room—to garden—to car —to market—to social powwows—and back indoors to his corner. He showed real enthusiasm for a ride in the station wagon from the first time we took him out to see the sights in our valley, and he celebrated the occasion with some real harmonious (for a change) singing. Even as we did our chores we rarely abandoned him to his own amusement until both broken bones had knitted and the top-of-head wound had scabbed over. Constant attention, joy rides, handling, and roughhouse games at last converted fear and loneliness into security and a form of familiarity that would have equated contempt in any other species.

Frankly, we had never before heard of anyone who had *roughhoused* with a bird!

Our foundling no sooner learned to eat without help than he decided it was more fun to be fed by human hand. He lapped up the ladle routine. For weeks he lowered his head and fluttered his fit wing, uttering high-pitched baby squeals, yelling to be hand-fed the moment we set a food bowl in front of him. With great relief we learned that if we tossed the ladle to the side of his bowl and walked away, he gobbled his groceries by himself. He caught onto drinking from a hummingbird gravity dispenser at an early date, because he sometimes choked and coughed when we squirted liquids down his Sunday throat with eye-dropper or water pistol. It wasn't that we were impatient; we were honestly unable to coordinate input volume of liquid with simultaneous output of vocal glut.

During his first month as our caged guest in the family den—with temperature thermostatically controlled and air filtered—the jay revealed behavior assumed to be native to his species. None of his increasing number of human friends could have predicted that any feathered creature would behave with such deliberate bad manners. Like a nest of Joyce Kilmer's robins, a jaybird in your hair requires neither poetry, photography, nor metaphor for an accurate mental picture of an accident looking for a *time* to happen (the place has already been established). While raising our jay, we acquired bad photos, unprintable metaphors, uptight mental pictures—and "accidents" that bordered on insanity.

It is safe to say that for eighteen months our bird's capers throughout the house and neighborhood exempted the community from any need for current news reports of violence, vituperation, vengeance, and volcanoes.

Talk about your firsthand experiences before writing! I recorded this story first on tape, then in a notebook, and finally on typed sheets while the blue jay chased my pen back and forth across handwritten pages or gawked in wonder from the carriage cover of my guano-encrusted typewriter. From the day our bird emerged from wing and leg splints, he coached and supervised my writing. His intimate presence never allowed a dull moment. If he seized a finished page and tore it up—as he often did—I typed it over. If he suspected that his destruction had gotten to me, he strutted and poured forth a running commentary of buzzy glee, looking forward to the next page—and possibly believing that *he* was amusing *me*.

Shoulder-borne during these first performances, he urged swifter production. If I offered him a blank sheet of paper, he hollered and pecked my hands.

Beaming from the clipboard that held my yellow writing pads, he "chuckled" while he "chattered." His fun was authentic; his "laughter" genuine; his motivation probably laced with incipient fraud.

Following his initial trauma, our blue jay grew and matured at an amazing rate. Not only did he become a member of the family, he also took over our lives. Once he was healthy and uninhibited, his fantastic potential unfolded by the hour. Our notebook record of him fell way behind if we missed so much as one day's entries.

2

AS THE JAY DEVELOPED, HE feathered out and demonstrated educated preferences for amusement, mischief, and dandyism. He reminded Lea of a notorious historical personage, Lorenzo de Medici—the Italian gent with enough loose coin to launch the Renaissance. Lorenzo the Magnificent they called him (to his face). According to his own files, Lorenzo patronized trickery, dupery, thievery, the other guy's *signora*—and Michelangelo. In many respects this sounded remarkably like our bird, and so Lea started calling him Lorenzo. When it took him four days to answer and come when called, I worried about his IQ. Then Lea reminded me that nimble-witted dogs require a week or more to respond to a name. Our Lorenzo may even have launched his own avian Renaissance. But because of his unsophisticated appetite, I still say he should have been called Pac-man.

Innate curiosity and the desire for closer relationships with his human associates soon brought the discovery that his cage had no door. With the aid of his off-center beak and one newly functioning wing—with serviceable pinions—he could hobble, hop, and climb like a parrot from solitary confinement to almost anything or anyone. Shortly after we removed his leg splints and the restrainer from his now-healed wing, he added several favorite landing strips: the breakfast table and the kitchen counter. Growing feistier by the hour, he then chose a lampshade and the curtain valance box in the den. The vocal bedlam he created in celebration of his sudden discovery that he could fly was described by a neighbor as "a brouhaha, if you wish to understate it!"

What Lorenzo chose as a landing strip, he kept. The curtain valance box presented a problem, at least for us. Recent inpatients—a mockingbird, two linnets, a cedar waxwing, and a white crown—had used the valance as a semiprivate, high-level latrine, and Lea had just finished reupholstering it when the wounded jaychick arrived. We wanted to keep the valance in its newly restored condition, and decided to decree it off limits for Lorenzo. By waving a small plastic flyswatter in front of his face we shooed him away time and again.

Lorenzo was not a *slow* learner; he learned only what he wanted to.

The flyswatter worked for a while. Then one night he prepared to contest our right to keep him off the valance, including in his plot the decision to test the physical effectiveness of the flyswatter. I should have become suspicious when he edged slowly over to my place on the sofa without ever taking his eye from mine. He quickly hopped to where I kept the flyswatter. Flaunting his grit, the nervy rascal seized the plastic swatter and dragged it to the center of the floor, where he scratched it cautiously with his talons, turned it over without drawing so much as a squirm of retaliation, finally gave it a good thrashing, puffed out his feathers, and shook himself. His ability to fight must have been hereditary.

Once his enemy was prostrate on the floor, Lorenzo flew to the valance box to establish squatter sovereignty with carefully timed vocal outbursts. When I nudged him lightly with the swatter, he fought back, "snarled," and refused to budge. After a week's persistence he finally demolished the plastic "tiger."

As a term of unconditional surrender, we tacked a polyester strip over the valance box. He often needled us thereafter by strutting from one end of the valance to the other in the hope, I am convinced, that we might try to evict him from that attractive perch . . . his victory had been too easily won. Something had to be wrong.

In addition to the valance box comfort station, we granted Lorenzo a floorlamp, the roost of his choice where he retreated with assurance of privacy and security from disturbance. Since the innovative days of our orphan mockingbird, Kaufman, other inpatients had found this safety roost to their liking and well-being. Despite his self-confidence, Lorenzo was a clinger. Since his favorite perch was the fabric shade of the floorlamp, we agreed never to violate that home port for any reason. Not even to confiscate contraband from his stealing forays.

If we happened to amble past the lampshade,

Lorenzo employed his version of "You can't come here!" with ruffled plumage and high-pitched "snarls." We soon learned to make a wide detour around his aerie. If he retreated to the safe place with dangerous objects in his mouth—razor blade, pin, scissors, or match—we had a problem. One of us had to coax him to another room with a bribe, while the other removed the forbidden loot Lorenzo had stored between the two towels with which we attempted to protect the shade. When he fussed later about missing property, we introduced an attractive substitute: chocolate fudge or a shiny new doodad without sharp edges.

On the desk in the den was a small lamp with a paper shade, an article that should have been thrown out months before—except that Kaufman, and later Lorenzo, took a shine to that lamp and its little red shade. At first Lorenzo was happy merely to stand under it, perhaps for the heat from the small bulb. Later on, however, he began to tear bits from the shade and eat them! Because he became more enchanted with the lamp as he matured, we left the shade for his eventual total consumption if he so desired.

That business of taboos must have puzzled him. If a blue jay could possibly ask, "Why?" Lorenzo certainly would have demanded—and rightly so—to know how it was that he could devour one lampshade, perch freely on another, yet was never allowed even a comfortable pause on a third.

Such confusion about taboos set in one night, causing him to leave the room. Lea had restrained the jay
from hammerheading her wristwatch. When he
brought me his lengthy complaint, I allowed him to
peck mine. Then I stopped him from carrying off my
eyeglasses, so he took that grievance to Lea, who let
him have hers! Next he flew to a chairback where he
studied both of us for a long time, staring first at me
then at Lea. As he flew away, he issued a new kind of
wail that seemed to say something about inconsistency.

One night I relieved him of a small finishing nail
he had discovered in a toolbox that I had carelessly left
open. Instead of throwing a tantrum after I took it
away from him, he flew to my knee with a technique
he and the mockingbird Kaufman had recently perfected in the backyard jungle: the cold, silent staredown. He had no doubt observed the telling effect of

this new performance on outdoor dwellers in the garden. Lorenzo's piercing gaze from my knee seemed to imply that I was a bigger thief than he only because of my size. He soon learned that getting what he wanted depended upon more subtle factors than who could outstare whom.

From his first day with us Lorenzo learned that his best goodies came from the human hand; therefore, his most intelligent early reactions were to our hands. Besides offering the easiest place to light on a person's body, the hand became a constant source of food, drink, rescue, amusement, information, companionship, and security. We saw to it that he associated voice tones as well as hands with basic necessities. Fingers were wonderful for pecking because they wiggled competitively and sometimes made infuriating noises as they tapped a variety of materials. Relating the voice-hand kinship with domestication, which we did not want, we took care never to indulge those activities to the extent that Lorenzo would have liked. We cannot recall the end of a play session with him when he didn't beg for more.

He detested hands that seized him, but of his own choice he loved to step up onto an extended finger, which he did with dignity and grace even before we removed his splints. The extended forefinger meant a free ride into the bathroom, study, or garden. He landed on my hand with a loud and rapidly uttered "story" whenever Lea raised the yardstick to shoo him off curtains or the dining room chandelier. Despite early chickhood scrapes with human meals in preparation, knitting basket, and freshly stacked clean linen, he looked to the hand for peace offerings. I hasten to add that no human hand ever punished him.

When we felt it was necessary to catch him, he did not always agree with our timing; accordingly, for his own good we were sometimes forced to outmaneuver him. One or another of the following methods usually did the trick:

1. We held out a hand and made kissing sounds, smacked whistles in reverse. We called his name. Ordinarily he landed and more or less surrendered unless he had cause to suspect dirty pool, such as confiscation of booty on the taboo list or the breaking up of a fight he was likely to win on the lawn.

2. We placed a finger against his breast and said, "Up!" He stepped up and clung for a ride or "conversation." He pecked hard if he thought we had broken any promise or had subdued him through deceit.

3. We just reached out and grabbed him when the other voice-hand appeals failed.

Together with voice, the human hand also served as a vital source of information and physical help, especially while his early wounds were healing. He was sometimes more leery of inanimate objects than of people or other animals: clocks that ticked, timers that ticked and then rang a bell, TV, refrigerator motor that went off and on. Strangers' hands provided flattery, food, and detachable jewelry. New animals (without grabbing hands or claws) were fun to chase and peck. Airborne creatures just out of range were even more enjoyable to tease; but every tool in the yard, strange "trinkets" on my workbench, shoelaces he had never untied, a strange car, a flowerpot—all had to receive an okay from our hands and voice before Lorenzo accepted them. Even then, they had to be tested. If an indoor nut was too hard to crack—and he really wanted the meat—he placed it gently upon an extended palm with lengthy "explanation." To his enduring credit, I must say, he rarely brought us a service problem without first having tried to solve it by himself.

He developed another impulsive habit: backing up and poking his newly feathered tail into our hands. Whether or not he did this ridiculous performance in order to get us to tug lightly, thus giving him cause for lively complaint, we had no way of knowing . . . and the library was indeed short of examples of that idiosyncrasy. He would repeat the gesture many times, then cluck like a setting hen when we honored his spoof. We have no idea what this behavior meant to him, but we felt we owed him his own few moments of nonsense.

Only once did the human hand unwittingly betray him. Thanks to his insatiable curiosity, Lorenzo automatically accepted anything offered by hand if he could carry it in his beak. I was sitting on the sofa one evening shortly after he had learned to fly. The folder of papers I was working on was held together by a rubber band. Without thinking of possible consequences, I handed the elastic to the jay, who was standing on my knee, eyeing the batch of papers, either wondering what I was doing or planning a possible snatch. He accepted the rubber band with a graceful bow and flew to the desk with it, perhaps suspecting that I might call back the donation of such an attractive piece of loot.

Holding down a segment of the rubber band with both feet, he began stretching the elastic back and forth by holding on with his beak. During these calisthenics, at the moment of farthest stretch—almost eight inches —Lorenzo somehow let go of his foothold. The rubber band did what rubber bands have been doing for a long time, and snapped the jay's lower mandible with such a jolt that he reeled half-conscious off the desk and plummeted into the wastebasket.

Blustering up a mini-storm with every feather at half-mast, Lorenzo flew to my hand and vented his rage by jackhammering my fingers until they were ready to bleed. Lea and I continued to snicker all evening, but the jay remained grumpy and returned periodically to punish the irresponsible hand that had dealt him the Sunday punch.

The next night we included the rubber band among his toys. I was eager to get his reaction to what he remembered. Scrappy as ever, he showed neither fear nor dislike when he delivered the elastic to me for safekeeping, but he was through forever with calisthenics.

For two weeks Lorenzo remained cagey about newspapers delivered with rubber bands around them. He called, with what I interpreted as a demanding tone, for me to test them before he accepted them. Having witnessed on many occasions the several dimensions of jaybird revenge, we accused the bird of trying to maneuver me into getting snapped on the chin. Without underestimating what could really happen after his misadventure, he seemed to enjoy the danger element along with the noise when I lifted and snapped rubber bands against paper. It was fun when my hand did the trick, but Lorenzo clung to the sidelines.

Rubber band snapping was definitely a spectator sport!

Just as contemplative curiosity wised up our bird about things that snapped, so the many attractive backyard temptations, often seen from the windows of the den during his convalescence, seemed to beckon now that he could run and fly. In the hollow of an ancient elm next to our patio lived Barnaby, a full-grown red squirrel, whose daily habit it was to knock on doors all over the block and panhandle nuts, popcorn, cookies, and dried fruit. Everybody knew and liked the silent Barnaby. For many hours, the squirrel had sat on the windowsill and gawked at the patched-up jaychick in the holding cage. As a former outpatient of ours, Barnaby had also acquired that avid curiosity so common for some reason among our releasees.

When Lorenzo stared back at Barnaby with un-

blinking black eyes, filling the stare with mystery and evil, the resourceful jay at an early age discovered that squirrels go bananas in the face of a cold staredown. Who can keep from looking back at any creature that stares? So, when he could catch Barnaby's eye, Lorenzo deliberately needled him into fits of squirrelly rage.

Also free-roaming in our backyard were assorted orphan outpatients who were reluctant to leave the home-sweet-smorgasbord that was available to all on feeding trays. Most visibly and vocally obvious of these was the aforementioned mockingbird who answered to our call of Kaufman. We named him after a family next door who complained that the bird sat regularly on their chimney at 3:00 A.M. and conjugated irregular Spanish verbs.

It may have been Lorenzo who taught Kaufman to needle Barnaby with the cold, deadly stare. Anyway, Kaufman had homemaking ideas of his own in the old elm high above Barnaby's apartment, which led to inevitable confrontations.

3

Dr. Elliott Coues, an early frontier student of birds, should have known Lorenzo and our backyard collection of boisterous blue jays. Said Dr. Coues: "The jay is a regular filibusterer, ready for any sort of adventure that promises sport or spoil, even if spiced with danger." He went on to describe jays as ". . . sharp, aggressive, and persistent, vain to their talon tips. Apparently jays are all but worry-free and therefore spend time on vanity that other birds cannot afford."

John James Audubon, writing about jays, said,

"Who can imagine that a form so graceful, arrayed by nature in a garb so resplendent, should harbor so much mischief?"

Further reading revealed that the word "jay" originated in vulgar Latin: *gaius,* went through old French as *geae,* pronounced something like our English *jay.* Besides more than two dozen species scattered throughout the United States, the blue jays' closest cousins—whiskey jacks and camp robbers (Clark's crows or nutcrackers)—range from northern Yukon Territory to the Central American hills. A related species lives in coastal brush along both coasts of Mexico. Bird watchers identify Lorenzo as *Aphelocoma californica:* California jay, scrub jay, bush jay. Take your choice. Our dashing specimen was really a natural inhabitant of chaparral and scrub-oak-covered hillsides and canyons. His immediate family lives in every Western state, the Southwest, and the Deep South to Florida. Most Corvidae (crow family) birds migrate only to the snowline in winter unless cold eliminates all food sources. Some don't bother to migrate except when fire threatens. Jays, magpies, nutcrackers, crows, ravens, and the related Mexican species—even birds of paradise—are all big-appetite cousins of a huge family under a variety of feathered skins.

Variety means evolutionary survival value. Jay instincts and characteristics reach back into the mists of time and have changed but little in millions of years.

Compared with most birds, jays are slow fliers. They poke along at a maximum of twenty MPH, rarely more than sixty feet above the ground. Hence, the jay is an easy mark for falcons that stoop (dive) at 150 MPH. But what the jay lacks in getaway speed he often makes up in maneuverability—unless he gets brash with a big hawk.

We watched a Steller's crested jay at Blue Jay (Lake Arrowhead), California, make a clumsy, diving pass to chase a Cooper's hawk away from the jay's nest. Stupid jay! He should have quit while he was ahead. Once the hawk enticed the jay out of the trees, the predator banked and poured on the fuel. The hawk taloned the jay in midair and carried the victim to a mountainside aerie.

We photographed jays gliding slowly under an osprey's nest in Yellowstone National Park to catch fish "crumbs" that fell from the extravagant predator's "table." Jays sometimes engage in a slow, awkward power dive . . . and they generally regret it.

My neighbor, who took up the trombone after hearing a month of arias by Lorenzo, claims that jays fly slowly in order to have enough breath for the noise they make while on the wing. Perhaps he is right.

Lorenzo learned the fine points of flight in less than a week after we removed splints and restrainer, but one clubbed foot still prevented his grasping normally;

therefore, in order to force toe exercises, we tricked him into landing on half-inch dowels. On these he had to cling for all he was worth to pull food, toys, and attractive no-nos from our fingers with his beak. At the same time the workout did much to reshape a distorted bill. Fortunately, he considered the activity a game. Blue jays, we read, love competitive athletics, particularly body-contact sports, as long as their win-syndrome is appropriately fueled.

During competitive exercise activities that he took as games, Lorenzo explored with careless abandon ways to communicate with us. At length he made us understand that assorted jaybird sounds and signals must be accompanied by specific body movements to have meaning. His hubbub and commotion translated into practical, if hazy, "vocabulary." A head bobbing up and down, accompanied by a metallic throat ratchet meant: "How about a swig?" Meaning milk, coffee, cocoa, juice, or beer . . . whatever I happened to be drinking. We interpreted repeated pecks on the hand in conjunction with "inflected" squawks as: "Gimme that!" Meaning whatever we had that he wanted. His communication signals lacked one thing only: *subtlety*.

Freedom to roam about the house reinforced a gnawing desire to seek—rather than demand—more human companionship, a tendency that later developed into the remarkable characteristic of aggressive loyalty. Lorenzo shot holes in the bird people's belief that he was too old for imprinting. He had arrived presumably too old to accept us as his family.

Not only did he accept us, he *abducted* us.

As one former jaybird owner put it: "If men wore feathers and had wings, very few would be clever enough to qualify as blue jays."

Lorenzo soon qualified. When his tail feathers grew to maximum development and his toes straightened, Lorenzo looked less like Pac-man on a food prowl. He swaggered about in his own methodical way on long jet-black legs and toes with fishhook talons. Fluffy gray feathers at last replaced baby down; his wings, the same bicycle-blue as head and tail, reached maturity in about six months. Every day he practiced new vocal numbers—a kind of precociously jarring jazz. Like Béla Bartók, he did everything possible to avoid harmony. He shifted into a semi-silent state only when he slept. Silence chez Lorenzo meant the low, enginelike sputter of an oil-thirsty chain saw. His rusty attempts to imitate Kaufman alerted us to administer cough syrup with an eyedropper for fear he had developed a respiratory disease as a result of San Fernando Valley smog. Our veterinarian assured us (for ten dollars), however, that a jaybird undergoes voice change when "pubic" plumage appears, followed by an exasperating period of adolescence, much in the manner of his human counterparts.

A dearth of literature on the subject defeated our lengthy search for a clue to recognize "pubic plumage."

One disturbed neighbor remarked, "Any change in that bird's voice would be for a better-off neighborhood."

Again in the manner of his human counterparts, Lorenzo grew up against his will. We frequently had to chase, shoo, or drag him to his sleeping quarters before he would retire for the night. When his tail feathers reached full length and his clubbed foot could perch, it was obvious that he needed more headroom in his chamber. For outdoor housing during the day, I built a large fly-around pen with chicken mesh on all sides—a kind of luxury holding cage until he was ready for complete freedom.

Along one side of the pen we established two army mess-hall-type stainless steel trays for his endless smorgasbord of preferred foods. At one end of the "nutrition counter" stood his water bowl, constantly freshened by a timed dripper. Certainly not for sanitary reasons, but because he had so much fun with it, we kept the floor of his coop covered with shredded newspaper. The cage also served admirably as a display case where local wildlife could peacefully make Lorenzo's acquaintance long before the day of his permanent release. The neighborhood simply had to brace itself before we turned the rogue loose.

Reluctant as he was to retire at night, he refused to sleep anywhere but inside the indoor cage where he had overcome chickhood handicaps. Ridiculously, he crammed himself into the smaller container designed originally for a hunch-backed canary. His morning exits, with frazzled feathers, from the little cell left him looking as if he had survived a shotgunning.

Not surprisingly, the first order of the day for Lorenzo was breakfast, often shared with his human friends. I'll never forget one morning when Lea shoved his drinking bowl in front of him on the kitchen table where the bird and I were still eating breakfast—from my plate. She thought his soft chur-ring was an out-of-character polite (for a change) request for a drink of water after having helped him-self to my bacon and eggs. To our surprise, Lorenzo hopped into the bowl, sat kerplop, stared us both down with his reptilian scowl, and took the sloppiest bath since kitchen washtub days of the last century. Stepping from his "tub" after five minutes, Lorenzo skipped, squawked, and skidded about the wet For-mica table top like a mechanical toy. He realized his inability to fly soaking wet, so he crept behind the table radio and squeegeed the water from each feather with his beak, creating a second-category mess.

Thereafter, like all jays we have observed, vain

Lorenzo reveled in his daily bath. He sat in the water from two to fifteen minutes, depending upon the weather or the big-business pressures he pretended to have scheduled for the day. First, he soaked his head and neck as if testing the water temperature. He liked it at 75° F. Then he stepped in, sat down, and shuffled the water upward through his wings. Whose problem was it if everything from ceiling to floor got soaked? There were two big humans to sponge up the flood after one jaybird's bath. Partly because he was afraid of a big local jay who used it, Lorenzo savored no kicks from a spacious birdbath located on the patio. And, too, no audience, no kicks.

When he stood on one spot and called immediately after breakfast, that meant: "Kindly place my tub here." He refused to bathe until we set the vessel—depending upon the day or his mood—on the tile counter, table, or linoleum. After bathing, he stepped haughtily from the water and expected one of us to dry him with a soft synthetic sponge.

Indoors or out, we submitted to his commands and practiced immediate response as a reward for his having communicated any real message.

Bona fide ornithologists soon declared that all Lorenzo's "unconventional" drives and messages were socially and culturally directed in terms of the rewards and punishments he received. Except for regular nighttime shutdown—which could not be considered a punishment—Lorenzo was punished only once, much later. With apologies to the ornithologists, we preferred to think of command and response as *the beginning of dialogue.*

Whether that dialogue involved a bath or a rooftop duet between Lorenzo and Kaufman, it very often approximated burlesque . . . the "harmony" of the two birds was not unlike what might be expected from an avalanche of empty tin cans. During his first inpatient days and the first months following his release, Kaufman had been a meek and gentle fellow. Then along came Lorenzo. The jay's influence began to undermine the mocker's gentility as soon as the two became friends—long before Lorenzo enjoyed full-time independence. Like Lorenzo, Kaufman began to squall about his exploits, most often at 3:00 A.M. when our fellow townspeople were inclined to be overcritical and a little unfair. Much later a neighbor claimed to have seen Kaufman and Lorenzo receiving handouts at the back door of a local taco parlor. This quite naturally led to the rumor about Kaufman and the Spanish conjugations.

Singing, we soon learned, was one of Lorenzo's favorite extracurricular activities. Of an evening indoors, he brought us a boiled-down rehash of his cage life in the backyard jungle. We sometimes sat for an

hour making notes, trying to distinguish among "tunes" of conquest, contentment, and condemnation. Of course, it was fantasy . . . we liked it that way after so many workaday realities.

Lorenzo and Kaufman took fanciful liberties with the songs of other creatures—as well as ego trips outside their own cultural landscape. Ostensibly, Kaufman did a better job imitating Lorenzo than our bird did trying to imitate Kaufman. But like mockingbirds, blue jays appear fascinated by the sounds of their own voices. While Kaufman sat on Lorenzo's big outdoor cage, they made sizzling steak sounds, gurgling hisses, and vocal exclamation points when other birds such as linnets, warblers, and meadowlarks interrupted the cacophony. *How* they sang was clear . . . *why* or *what* the racket accomplished may have involved subtleties of territorial proclamation. Like the rattling of buck deer antlers, stridency may have reflected the *desirability* of those two bachelors.

When sparrows gossiped from Fig Leaf Towers (our huge fig tree that hid many a nest), Lorenzo blew his yodel horn, notes very much like a referee's whistle. The blast usually silenced the sparrows, and during the lulls, Lorenzo and Kaufman could reproduce a frog's croak, a cricket's hoarse whisper, or a cicada's file-and-scraper music. As might easily be assumed, the jay cut his best figure imitating the cicada.

4

BOTH LORENZO AND KAUFMAN LEARNED every note of their inter-urban bel canto without coaching of any kind, a remarkable phenomenon in self-teaching.

Like the spider that spins the ancestral web, or the oriole that weaves the family basket nest, neither creature had an ancestral model. To my knowledge the mocker and the jay never did find a reason to sing the same tune in the same key at the same time. My trombone-playing neighbor stated flatly: "The bees will learn to bark before those two loud-mouthed birds learn to sing!"

The *very young* Lorenzo was not embarrassed when we laughed at his singing. In fact, he seemed to solicit laughter unless he happened to be composing "mood music," the kind that disturbs the background of otherwise good TV programs. Lorenzo apparently was the composer of most of his opuses, because we never once heard another jay sing a similar tune. In fact, they all sang different "tunes." Our jay was polishing up the refrain of such a song one afternoon when a young student of bird behavior (with the unlikely name of Red Underbeak) arrived to take notes on our remarkable bird. When the jay "sang" and "danced" at the same time on a perch inside his fly-around coop, the young man doubled up with laughter. Underbeak was unaware that "dancing" was Lorenzo's signal for the student to knock off the giggles.

Underbeak accepted my explanation that laughter annoys jays under certain rare circumstances. You learn the difference by living with them. Many animals, wild and domestic, react negatively to human laughter, especially when they recognize themselves as the target and when they are being serious. Lorenzo was extraordinarily sensitive about people's intentions. Although he was loathe to yield the spotlight even when the joke was on him, there were times when he demanded sober-mindedness.

"Why doesn't he just shut up or fly away to his own

private concert stage?" Underbeak asked. "The door is open."

"He rarely stops singing until he comes to the end of a melody," I said. "Even if I pick him up and carry him to the house, he generally sings till he finishes what he has started. Kaufman was never that way. He stopped the minute we picked him up. He sometimes stopped if we just looked at him.

"Let's step back and look around. He's up to something when he tunes in like a leaky faucet and ends with a foghorn rasp. I'd bet he's toying with a problem hereabouts."

We had no sooner stepped back than Barnaby's mate descended the acacia near the back fence and leaped to the threshold of Lorenzo's cage. Within moments the jay tossed peanuts and raisins through the doorway. With the goodies from this offering stored in cheek pouches, the squirrel looked as though she had the mumps. The two wildlings bowed in the manner of Japanese nobility. And then the squirrel hastened back up the acacia, where we saw six little squirrel heads peering over the side of a twig-thatched nest high above.

It seemed that nettlesome Lorenzo had sung for a charitable cause! On occasion he could present a somewhat out-of-focus picture of generosity . . . provided he had an audience of enthusiastic applauders.

Underbeak wanted to write an article on what

makes blue jays sing or yell in so many different ways, pitches, keys, and tones. Who can honestly say? I cited only what we had observed. Lorenzo sang when other creatures sang . . . or when they were silent. No doubt he sang as other birds do: to proclaim territorial rights. It appeared that he sang inside his cage for the deliberate purpose of disturbing other creatures that drowsed away a long summer afternoon. He sang and "danced" when I came home after shopping, and again for reasons of mimicry, just before dark—especially when evening toads and crickets tuned up. We interpreted most of his vocal output as exuberance directed toward specific activities. But we have also heard jays utter mournful dirges following the loss of their nestlings to predators.

Lorenzo gargled a vigorous accompaniment to virtually all canned music: a rusty hinge (man, how that did turn him on!), a toilet flush, a Schubert symphony. His tastes were catholic. There was a stage in his development when he bubbled out sharps and flats with equal glee whether he perched on human finger or the apical bud of a pine tree across the street. But unless the mood for song prodded the bird, nothing could force him to crack a note. His melodies seemed cockier by day than by night, possibly because outdoor competitors offered more challenge between dawn and sunset.

When he stole a sip of sacramental wine, we feared he might stagger into a break-dance.

It was of lively significance that, as a growing bird, he loved to be laughed at in everything but song and bath.

Speaking of Lorenzo's songs recalls to mind a package of small, foreign-smelling seeds purchased for one of our linnet outpatients. According to advertising claims on the package, those seeds would wring song from the most backward horned toad. Never having known a backward problem with Lorenzo, we nonetheless were forever trying ways to improve the quality of his song. Blue jays are not seed eaters in the strictest sense. But good sport that he was, Lorenzo sampled whatever grain we offered. Judging by the embarrassing fact that his vocal output suddenly multiplied several times, he may have relished the linnet chow. Although improvement in pitch, range, key, or tone was far to the left of negative, Lorenzo's evening ramblings, after a "song-seed" meal, seemed more loaded than usual with recountable adventures. Shortly after finishing the package of little black seeds, our jay's finest hour reached its thirty-minute zenith: his song in a farkleberry bush broke up a flute, bassoon, and trombone chamber trio!

To get the jay in a singing mood, sometimes we set the stage by crumbling foil, rattling pebbles in an empty coffee can, tuning the radio on rock-and-roll, or when all else failed, bringing out the rusty hinge.

On occasion we succeeded in priming his "artistry" by whistling "Oh Susannah!" or by rendering "La Paloma" on the harmonica. But next to the Rolling Stones, chili-con-carne jazz, and chopped liver, the mysterious seeds produced the most sensational serenades. When I taped Lorenzo's warblings, and played them back later, he flew to a small mirror on Lea's dressing table and charged his reflection, apparently believing that another jay was the singer. Getting nowhere with direct frontal attack, he ran around behind the looking glass to sneak up on the plagiarizer. Finding no jay, he skipped the whole thing in favor of a ladybug on the windowsill. That way he could still pretend to feed his win-syndrome, unless I set the tape in motion again. In such a case, he sat in a corner and went quietly off his rocker.

He never sat for very long. Within the time frame of one day that Lorenzo was allowed outside his coop to explore the backyard and a few fellow wildlings, he learned to extract a peanut from its shell, to exterminate a slice of bread (without having to eat it), to yank an uncooperative earthworm from a flower bed, and to harmonize—after a fashion—with Kaufman, who accompanied him on his first day of experimental freedom. The mockingbird habitually hung out either among the ripe fruit in Fig Leaf Towers, on the ridgerow of our roof, or on the top of Lorenzo's coop.

At the end of eight weeks of increasing independence, we bragged about Lorenzo's wing and leg nor-
malcy. Instead of hobbling and shrieking about the
house, he *flew* and shrieked. After an additional
month's daily therapy—to which he objected with
such a ruckus that we were reported to the SPCA—
his tangled toes untwisted to the degree that he could
grasp almost any perch. His back toes still didn't an-
chor well, but in time he learned either to compensate
or to cling tighter up front. We zinc-oxided his bald
head to keep him from contracting the roup on chilly
nights or sunstroke when he followed us out-of-doors.
His crooked beak still gave him the royal Spanish
Hapsburg look: Charles V, Phillip II, etc.

Despite an early addiction to mischief, Lorenzo
grew into an affectionate, cuddly being, happiest when
he could perch and coo for an hour on a human
shoulder before goodnight time. His cooing sounded
exactly like two pieces of coarse sandpaper rubbed
together in an empty rain barrel. With devilish speed
he caught on to the fact that affectionate cuddling
succeeded in delaying bedtime. He also discovered in
both of us the original sucker-bait; consequently, he
played his underhanded role to the hilt whenever he
plotted to topple one of our familiar routines. Like his
predecessors, Lorenzo was self-taught, of course, in
educational activities that involved the fine points of
flying, singing, or deceiving. Remember, this bird

came to us with shattered wing bones, broken leg, clubbed foot, peeled scalp, and twisted beak! Instead of dropping out of the air when he wanted to stop, he learned, no doubt from Kaufman, to alight gracefully by extending his legs for purchase and by tilting his pinions and tail feathers as air brakes. In other words, in flying and singing he learned to imitate rather than learn by imitation, although some will say that he learned to deceive from his ancestors. Shrill squawks that issued from his vocal cords at every landing led one imaginative visitor to call him NASA, because his mouth and lungs acted as retrorockets to slow him down.

By the time he moulted his baby down, pinfeathers plagued Lorenzo. Through scratching, he achieved skill with initially clumsy claws, toes, and bill. We began to suspect an infestation, so I wrestled him down one night and sprinkled his wingpits and legpits with pyrethrum powder. You should have seen his mercury rise! Two days later I was still begging pardon—still unforgiven—for the needless indignity. That bird made me understand that blue jays are *not* lousy. He punished me with vicious beak yanks, hammerhead pecks, and scathed me with new "vocabulary" that I suspected he had picked up from Kaufman's sparrow buddies. In addition, Lorenzo perfected the dark, reptilian scowl.

My drastic handling of the jay's scratching may

have launched his life-for-fun career that followed, because from that day on, I believe he decided not merely to *endure* life but to *enjoy* every minute to the fullest—on his terms. He taxed his own creative imagination in a perpetual quest for joy. Many of his deeds may have been instinctive rather than willful; nevertheless, people who have raised blue jays told us that the species definitely inclines toward the credo of eat, drink, and caper today . . . you might change your mind tomorrow.

When he was brought indoors of an evening, he rarely just entered the den; he invaded it. Between supper time and sleep time, he really took over. In the first place, it was unusual for him to show any effects of fatigue, so when he learned to fly, he regrooved our evening rut formerly devoted to reading, writing, discussing, TV, or just relaxing after a hard day's work. Most birds we had raised either flew to our shoulders, to a door top, or to the curtain valance until they got their bearings. Not Lorenzo. Our house had become part of his territory. Immediately upon entering the den, he dropped to the center of the floor, cocked an expressive head and tail, did half a dozen rapid push-ups, stiff-legged a couple of circles, shuttled his head and shoulders back and forth as if testing security, then settled on a landing target for further reconnoitering—customarily his lampshade.

If the room was full of people, he went through a similar routine but added long "Flacks!" Recognizing "his folks" instantly in a crowded room, he flew either to Lea's shoulder or mine, gawking from person to person and shrieking to drown out any other sounds in the room.

He developed an unusual fixation toward certain items in the den. Rare indeed is the creature that even notices objects not immediately associated with basic needs of food, shelter, or rest; yet most articles in our den—and in other rooms—either personally attracted or repelled Lorenzo. He never asked permission to seize or destroy an item. He simply seized and destroyed cut flowers, *blue* objects of any kind, typewritten pages, or newly acquired knickknacks that did not appeal to him or were not filchable. Oddly enough, he never destroyed genuine flowers out-of-doors.

Most to be deplored were items he could neither steal nor destroy.

During snoopy forays, he checked his hiding places or chose new booty to hide. Sometimes he chose new hiding places for everything! This may have depended upon whether he had met "relatives" during the day out-of-doors; at any rate, his sense of trust received a shock from such encounters. When all systems in the den were comfortably under his control, he flew to the desk and leisurely regarded what he probably considered his very own. By then it was time to turn a quiet, reflective gaze toward the sofa for a hint that would indicate human attitude or mood of the day. We think he had a scale for rating our daily household temper. He seemed to screen the family climate carefully and quickly through his built-in computer before deciding upon a specific looting technique or other behavior he might expect to get away with.

When other jays tucked their heads under their wings shortly after sundown, our bird—who had courted adventure since breakfast—was just beginning a four-hour rough-and-tumble competition in the house. Aware of the sheer joy he took from those evenings and the extra edge it gave him over his wild confreres, we rarely denied Lorenzo his share of fun and wonder.

When he was brushed off—physically—a dozen

times or more, he returned and stayed with a project until more attractive spoils captured his attention. He had a bulldog's tenacity for hanging on . . . without a bulldog's occasional willingness to mind. He often worked on my pipe with side glances at my eye that kept him under surveillance, as if he expected an explosive "No!" Not only did he have the unmitigated nerve to peck us on the nose, he had the guts to announce his intentions ahead of time.

Lorenzo rarely left a room. He executed shrill and forceful theatrical exits—unless silence was imperative to his next project, or unless he suffered wounded feelings. The bright-blue flash of his wings and his sparkling nonstop chatter brought gaiety, color, sound, and movement for which we gladly surrendered the quiet, post-Kaufman formalities. Without attributing to Lorenzo an impossible inventory of human characteristics, I could swear he knocked himself out to bridge the evolutionary gap between man and jay.

Much of his delinquent behavior and constantly new devices for devilment left little doubt that Lorenzo was training for a career as a lovable buffoon. Early signs of this trait showed up in his gusto for inventing boisterous games. I'll confess he received coaching each time he put the polishing touches on a new kind of hide-and-seek. First he "chuckled" when he disappeared into a darkened room where he hid behind or under furniture. If our search was not diligent enough to challenge his patience or if we gave up, he uttered a soft whisper, a hint, if you please. Next, a mandible clicked or a tail feather moved ever so slightly. If we exposed him unfairly by switching on a light, he would fly to the top of my head and pull my hair. When we found him honestly, he flew back to the den and "screamed" until one of us hid. When he was "It" he cheated regularly by peeking and listening while we tried to hide. No matter where we crawled or what secret door we closed behind us, Lorenzo had no trouble locating us. His hearing was so acute that he could pinpoint our breathing at twenty feet.

During the hide-and-seek game (his favorite amusement), we observed that he flew and landed with equal coordination in lighted or darkened rooms. One night he hid so well we could neither find him nor elicit a hint. An hour passed before we peeped into a closet and found him squatting, sound asleep in one of my shoes.

Most species, including *Homo sapiens,* play when time and strength remain after fulfilling the mandates of earning a living, but careful research and observation disclosed that blue jays play about 82 percent of their waking hours. Thus, they eat better, live longer, and enjoy life more than most creatures. For the jay, fun comes first even at the expense of losing a worm.

We think Lorenzo's habit of hiding what he was unable either to eat or to destroy was an inherited trait, because he stole and hid long before he ever saw another jay do the same thing. He could hide a peanut half in your shoe with such quick dexterity you might not have guessed it was there until you started to walk away. Hiding things has to be an evolutionary trait with jays. Survival value.

It was also noteworthy that Lorenzo hailed toys that rolled: corks, balls, toilet paper cores, and small bottles. He stood on the "rollers," got them in motion with beak and talons, flapped his wings for do-it-yourself, made-to-order scooter kits. By outfitting him with two dozen such toys, we sometimes kept him more or less disinterested in taboo areas: electrical appliances, medicine cabinet, and fireplace (where he buried some of his top treasures anyway, even when the ashes contained live coals).

On occasion we tested his alertness by withholding one of his twenty-four playthings. Carefully he went over the hoard three or four times before flying to one of us, pecking hands until welts arose, grinding out his loudest and graveliest wail on our shoulders, abusing us mentally and physically until we produced a missing bottle cap, button, safety pin, ballpoint, or tinklebell. In his outdoor cage he proclaimed robbery in tones audible for a city block if any changes of toys occurred. Unless immediately hooked by a new toy, however, he required the test of time before accepting new goodies out-of-doors.

Thinking always of toys for Lorenzo, we were often at wit's end for variety in bottle caps, stoppers, jar lids, small spoons, pencils, buttons, dime-store jewelry, large nails, and plastic models of smaller dollhouse furnishings. We altered the inventory often, estimating the playtime he would devote to each article before hiding it permanently. Once hidden, loot seemed to lose most of its entertainment worth. Still it was stored, accumulated wealth.

In spite of our vigilance, Lorenzo made off with

taboo items from Lea's sewing table: anything jay-portable. The only security was a lock and key. Sometimes we ignored him when he swiped valuable property. If we fussed up a storm and tried to recover an item from his beak, the object's asking price and desirability for him soared. Sometimes he escaped into the yard to hide "hot" boodle in a tree or under a shrub. The things he buried were seldom recovered. Taboo articles were worth any amount of effort in the eyes of the jay.

Jaybird thievery, like that of raccoons and crows, appears to be a trait of some practical value to the bird. So, you live with it. Such an ancient, lively art apparently cannot be trained out of wildlife swindlers. Try teaching a trade rat not to trade. Our problem became serious because of Lorenzo's genius for finding new hiding places with which we were unfamiliar and because of the increasing fun he experienced in larceny.

We used a tiny, expensive pair of German scissors

in delicate jobs of surgery we had to perform from time to time on wildlings. We kept that tool where Lorenzo's probing beak could never reach . . . or so we thought. When an emergency arose one day, the scissors were not to be found. Climb-the-wall-time! For "safe-keeping," Lorenzo often deposited his cargo in a wastebasket. Accordingly, we combed the garbage cans where wastebaskets had been emptied. No scissors. A week passed before I had occasion to refer to an encyclopedia. As I opened the volume, the scissors fell to the floor.

Most species eventually give up fun and frolic for the more serious business of earning a living. Not so the jaybird. Impervious to assaults of conscience and human expectations about mature behavior, the jay keeps most of his youthful attitudes throughout his ten- to-fifteen-year life span. His durability to with-stand shock, like his pursuit of happiness, allows him to claim victory where other species would certainly yell calamity and fold up. For example, we observed a pair of jays who kidnapped, adopted, and raised another nestful of jaychicks after their own fledglings had fallen prey to a weasel. Thus, by wit-minus-scru-ples, so it appeared, they gleaned happiness from trag-edy. The parents whose fledglings were abducted left our neighborhood, so we could only speculate as to how they felt about it.

5

L ORENZO BECAME AN EXPERT AT SAILING
over hurdles when it came to getting what he wanted.
With a tray of assorted jay treats in one hand and
Lorenzo in the other, Lea was transferring him one
morning to his outdoor coop where he could eat in
relative peace and at the same time watch his early-
morning world go by. For his own protection, he
wasn't yet allowed free flight between the house and
his garden quarters except on special occasions when
it looked as if he might cooperate. For several recent
renegade acts deliberately committed while free-

flying, he was not considered a good probation risk on the morning in question.

Suddenly appearing to forget his impatience for breakfast, Lorenzo broke loose and flew away. We heard Kaufman and him upsetting the peaceful balance of nature for a two-block radius. Since it was Lorenzo's first long flight away from home base, we feared he might not get back to his cage before outraged winged creatures descended upon his bald head. Two hours later he charged home with jays, towhees, and thrashers in hot pursuit. One indignant crow was within a yard of his tail feathers when Lorenzo popped into his cage. The cocky jay turned around and vented the "vocabulary" he had probably accrued for just such an occasion.

Standing with legs wide apart within the safety of his enclosure, he gulped Spam, prune whip, and overripe *quiche aux tomates.* He chased the heavies with Hawaiian Punch, then pretended to ignore his frustrated pursuers now perched and fussing in the trees overhead. Lea and I had been looking forward to the day when Lorenzo could lead an independent life in that same community, and we were therefore concerned about his apparent misbehavior during his two-hour AWOL. Birds, like elephants and Missouri mules, have long memories. To an individual so completely devoted to amusement, the whole affair must

have appeared deliriously funny. When he had gobbled up his breakfast, he whetted his beak on a perch,
then added his own voice to the backyard bedlam.
There was a sudden silence in the trees, and we de-
duced that Lorenzo must have delivered a forceful
"speech," especially when Lea closed his cage door and
snapped the lock, something we had not done for some
time because he was so good about staying inside the
coop until permitted out.

As we evaluated his morning escapade in the notebook we kept on Lorenzo, we mentioned our anxiety
about his crooked beak.

"How will he ever catch a bug with a mouth that
never completely closes?" I said to Lea the next day
as we watched him chase a butterfly across the lawn.
She thought his off-center beak was the cause of his
marathon mischief. Defense mechanism or compensa-
tion in people.

Still studying beak action, we sat one evening on
the sofa in the den and watched Lorenzo parry with
his "pet" Mexican jumping bean (we've known several San Fernando Valley families with pet Mexican
jumping beans). A small moth flew toward the reading
lamp on my desk. Far quicker than the eye, the jay was
airborne, the insect dead between his upper and lower
bill segments. Lorenzo flew back to my knees, swaggered up to my hand on the writing pad, and presented

me with the trophy. Reclaiming the moth later on, however, he swallowed it, then resumed his "duel" with the jumping bean.

Our fears about the crooked beak were obviously unfounded. As might be expected in Lorenzo's case, more complicated mouth-work was to follow. His favored toy of the moment was the opener-ring from a soft drink can. Two nights later the bird sailed around the room, looking for a place to hide the shiny hardware from imaginary thieves. A mosquito flew toward the lamp. Spotting the insect immediately, Lorenzo dived in for the catch, but just as suddenly, he remembered the metal opener between his mandibles. Before the mosquito could escape, the agile bird transferred the opener-ring to a foot, and with a loud mandible snap, grabbed the mosquito. For some time he flew first to Lea then to me, then around the den with his problem. He could not risk alighting with the opener in the talons of his good foot (the unclubbed one) and dared not open his beak lest he lose the mosquito wiggling inside his mouth. Finally he resolved his problem in midair. He swallowed the insect and at the same time dropped the opener-ring. For a long time he stood beside his toy in the middle of the floor and looked at Lea and me, as if considering his perfect solution to a serious equation. Long after that incident we were told that nonpredatory birds whose feet have recovered from certain damage often learn to clutch objects almost as predators do.

Whereupon we quit worrying about Lorenzo's off-center equipment—and his IQ.

After observing firsthand so many of our jaybird's antics, we chanced to read some fanciful yarns about blue jays. One author insisted the jay could distinguish about two dozen different colors. Recalling that the Munsell Color System lists only ten color families, we wondered if that writer hadn't soared a bit—got carried away, so to speak—on jaybird wings of enthusiasm. The article went on to emphasize that jays went ape over blue. Well, as I have tried to point out, Lorenzo was different. The scholarly reference made sense, in a way, until we placed four small plastic balls of different colors on the carpet. The blue one was a dead ringer for Lorenzo's blue head, wings, and tail. Which one did he charge, peck, and refuse to play with? The *blue* one, of course.

When we placed red, yellow, orange, green, and blue ribbons on the sofa, he picked all but the blue for his ribbon cache, chattering his loudest "loot talk" as he flew away to hoard the strips. He came back and tried to destroy the blue. Repetition of the experiment at two-day intervals for the next ten days yielded exactly the same results. He either ignored, pecked, or scolded the blue. All of which had the earmarks of a reasonable conclusion: Lorenzo turned up his beak at blue. I shall not set up a scientific experiment with 1,000 blue jays in order to document Lorenzo's monkeyshines.

Except for turquoise, which he ignored because it veered toward blue, you can imagine the fun Lorenzo had when unsuspecting visitors arrived wearing easily detachable jewelry. His dusky eyes took speedy inventory—raked and judged a client in one sharp glance. When he narrowed the slits between his eyelids, there was no mistaking his intention. If the combination of a small brooch, lapel pin, or earring stymied his skill, he poured on personal charm until the conned guest accepted a peanut or shiny tinklebell as security for a "loan." More important Lorenzo played for keeps ... like a slippery pro, he found his way around locked doors and windows when he was transporting valuables. Serious losses sometimes resulted from loans to the wicked but irresistible Lorenzo. We warned our guests that the jay had no conscience and that we assumed no responsibility for his "deals."

In consequence we learned that one of the healthiest conditions in a blue jay's life is competition; whether it originates during human custody or during association with feathered peers doesn't seem to matter. Variety, bluff, theft, snobbery, and attention-getting span several competitive fields. Food, toys, potential mates, and license to peck the other fellow also involve natural competitive elements in the jay's total psyche. Vain Lorenzo often preened his feathers, expanded his chest by overinhaling, then strutted before us like a drum major on parade. He went through the same studied motions for a bevy of unattached jayhens who happened to pop into the backyard when our jay was on display. As a suburban male sex symbol, Lorenzo made Burt Reynolds look effeminate.

When another jay challenged Lorenzo's *machismo,* our pretender hackled out his feathers, lowered his voice several octaves, and put on a good imitation of a chicken hawk while staring at the other jay—from behind the sturdy chicken mesh of his fortress. Each time he bumped into a familiar jay he knew he could not fight or bluff off the premises, he made his rudeness appear accidental. At least, it seemed that way. The result was always the same: a mock squabble where not more than two or three pecks were exchanged before Lorenzo could scoot to the safety of his aviary.

As one might prematurely conclude, Lorenzo sometimes overplayed his role as backyard pirate. He strong-armed smaller birds; by virtue of a tougher beak and sharper talons, he seized their chattels whether he wanted them or not. When he stole from birds his own size or bigger, his orderly, well-planned getaway seemed to suggest that he *sought* trouble and regretted not finding enough of it.

Utterly mystifying Lea and me at times, he chose

special occasions for a different role. When he looked for affection or approval, he came to our shoulders, sat down gently, fluttered his wings, and turned on the "whispering charm." The act reeked of fraud, especially if I had just bestowed attention upon a neighbor's parakeet or handed Kaufman a meal worm. Lea bugged him, but good, when she tossed grain to linnets and sparrows in our many-storied Fig Leaf Towers. As a matter of almost daily habit before the display of "whispering charm," the jay planted his six ounces of weight squarely on the ground at the nose of a friend's cocker spaniel and dared the dog to advance. The good old mutt simply winced, absorbed Lorenzo's peck, and sidestepped the jealous nuisance.

On one such occasion we saw Lorenzo skip the "whispering charm" gimmick. For once he was stumped at the feet of a jayhen who appeared not to be impressed by his display. The trouble, it soon turned out, was that the jayhen had a mate who was eavesdropping behind a curtain of foliage while Lorenzo tried to make out. The big jay was a bully whose revenge extracted a terrible price from Lorenzo in neck feathers and bill bruises. All Alphas in nature are by their very position bullies. Whoever heard of a benevolent Alpha?

By this time, whether engaging in a little harmless flirtation, in a squalid scam, or in downright strong-arming, Lorenzo had to learn never to underestimate strange blue jays. Each romantic effort had to be launched on an individual basis and not by formula. He got one picture clearly straightened out, and never went after another jay's hen unless he was sure of his own superior strategy of offense and defense.

During that first summer, Lorenzo gained further valuable awareness. From the beginning my pipe fascinated him. He often dropped like a bullet to my wrist to watch me fill and light the smelly old smudge-pot. He wiped out smoke rings with his wings. That appeased his win-syndrome! Whether he chased smoke or stole property, his movements became so fast that he generally finished a project before we had time to investigate what he was up to. Pretending to watch me one night in the den, he clung to the edge of my tobacco pouch while I filled the pipe. Then suddenly he dipped inside the container, seized a greedy mouthful of tobacco, and took off before I could grab him and choke it from his beak. When I finally caught him, the fool swallowed the tobacco rather than surrender it. Within ten minutes I had forgotten the fracas . . . it was so mild compared to some. Lorenzo, however, became unnaturally quiet. He sat hunkered over the top edge of his lampshade and hung his head.

"Lorenzo," Lea said, "you're too quiet. Are you all right?"

Whereupon the jay leaned forward, opened his

beak, and vomited the tobacco along with his supper.

Five minutes later he perked up and resumed his mischief. But from that day on, he was satisfied to perch on my wrist and *watch* while I filled my pipe.

As a young bird, Lorenzo considered it no sissy sport to clutch my old typewriter carriage and ride the noisy, old-fashioned mechanism back and forth as I typed page after beak-tested page. Then along came the shinier, faster, more complicated electric machine with automatic carriage return. The first time he attempted to ride that speedy new conveyor, he was smashed against the wall, from which he dropped to the floor with a dull thwack. He shook his head, perhaps persuaded that he had been guillotined. Thereafter, from the safety of my shoulder, he sat and "shouted" at the noisy typewriter.

Whether machine, coin, or can opener, metal objects continued to ignite Lorenzo's immediate curiosity, more so than nonmetallic hardware. Copper

interested him. So he took every penny he could "find." Silver in the form of dimes and quarters enchanted him. He collected gold in any form. The night he learned to crawl into my pocket and I allowed him to "lift" money was the time I goofed. Shortly afterwards, he performed a slick pickpocket act upon an insurance salesman with little knowledge of blue jays . . . and *no* sense of humor. As the bewildered man left, he mumbled something about a "trained specialist."

To all creatures given over to mischief, emergencies and tight squeezes must be a way of life. No one on such close terms with trouble as a jaybird could possibly reach maturity without picking up a scar or two. Because Lorenzo learned to strike kitchen matches with his powerful hammerhead chiseling, matches went pronto onto the taboo list. And because of the taboo, matches became at once worthy of grand strategy. The first one Lorenzo ever struck on the desk singed his mustache, sizzled one side of his beak, caused a spectacular pratfall, and burned a hole in the carpet. The desk top needed refinishing anyway.

Looking always for ways to soften Lorenzo's disappointments and crunches, we cut off the business ends of several wooden matches, placed them in a desk drawer, and left it partially open to see what would happen. Within moments the jay was circling the room with a matchstick between his mandibles, gargling a "victory song" in his own key. When he interpreted one of my moves as a chase, he swallowed the matchstick. Like a deflating balloon, he collapsed almost instantly onto the desk where he began to choke. While he struggled for breath and gasped through open mouth, I reached down his throat with a pair of blunt-nosed tweezers and pulled out the matchstick.

To demonstrate his profound appreciation for my having saved his life, Lorenzo pecked my hand viciously and spent the next ten minutes on his lampshade where he gave me the silent, iguana scowl treatment.

Lorenzo rarely blamed Lea for the salt in his wounds. I was a convenient target for his wrath because I monkeyed around with him more than Lea did. He may also have recalled that Lea had prepared his original F.F.F.F. We witnessed numerous examples of Lorenzo's "selective" appreciation.

One night Lea was concentrating on her magazine, paying as little attention to Lorenzo as he would tolerate—misplaced confidence, given that the bird was squatting on her chest, nibbling her blouse, and fumbling with a brooch. This obvious pre-performance ploy caused me to issue a strong "Ahem!" As Lea's story reached an exciting climax, she began chewing her gum more actively. A thrust of greased lightning could not have been much faster than the jay as his beak shot between Lea's teeth and grabbed her gum. Before we could catch him, Lorenzo had the gum stuck to both feet, mandibles, and feathers. Everything he touched clung to the gum: pins, string, paperclips, hair. At last he dove for the floor where he stood gummed to the shag rug, scowling his darkest indictment first at Lea, then at me. He clucked for help in a way that made both of us feel like heels for laughing at him and not rendering immediate help. Still, in all his obvious embarrassment, he surrendered not one iota of independence, arrogance, or impudence. So we brought out the several solvents, which included naphtha, glycerine, detergents, olive oil, and cold cream, along with Q-tips, tweezers, and toothpicks.

Have you ever tried to remove chewing gum from an objecting blue jay's mouth, feet, and feathers?

You wouldn't believe it!

I finally went to the ice cream parlor in the shopping center and bought dry ice to crumble the gum from his tail feathers.

6

Not long after the chewing gum fiasco, we were in the kitchen one morning cooking breakfast. Lorenzo stood on my shoulder, shifted his weight continually from one foot to the other, and dug his long, sharp talons through my shirt and into the flesh. That was his signal of complaint because I was frying the bacon much too slowly to suit his impatience and appetite. Whenever we had bacon, he demanded—and got—two half-slices: half-slices chopped up to extend gulping time. There was nothing he liked better than bacon, not too fat, not too lean, not too crisp, not too fresh.

On this particular morning, he suddenly hopped down and landed on the hot skillet handle, thus discovering with a shrill whoop one more taboo. After standing a few moments in a dish of ice water that Lea quickly set out for him, he flew back to my shoulder and glared down at the skillet, hissing his sulkiest "mad talk." Before I could stop him, he glided to the stove's edge and poked his head under the skillet to see where all that heat came from. It took two months for his long, black mustache to grow back and for the much-salved blister around his nostrils to heal. But he learned to shun flames, including those in the fireplace and the barbecue brazier. Survival value. Numerous jays without sufficient fear of fire are killed annually in California brush fires.

With or without pain and scars, the jaybird mystique—life for fun and fun for life—is indeed real. When Lorenzo reached what we estimated to be adolescence, we pitched a party and invited some of his favorite human fans to what one guest called a *jaybird Bar Mitzvah.* Among the goodies, all strong preferences of Lorenzo, we served sacramental wine and lox and bagels. Toward the end of the party, Lea located the suddenly "missing" Lorenzo on the kitchen counter, where he was nipping away at the dregs in the wine glasses. At a call, everyone rushed in to witness a feathered creature plastered to the hilt. His boozy squawk sounded like a tape recording played at too slow a speed. Reeling backwards along the counter, Lorenzo fell heels over appetite into a sink half-full of sudsy detergent. While I held him under the faucet, he "mumbled" feebly and pecked his own toes.

I set the bird on the linoleum floor because I dared not let him try wet wings in his condition. Lea placed a mirror in his path so he could see what he looked like. It was one of those magnifying mirrors men use when they trim a pencil-line mustache. Through droopy eyelids, our wet and miserable Lorenzo took

one squinty look, staggered backwards, and crumpled into a fluttering heap of slow-motion blah! Caged immediately, he looked even worse.

Next morning he made not the wheeziest peep. Once more our adventurous bird had acquired practical knowledge. I was ashamed to call the vet for aspirin information, revealing that Lea and I were nursing a bird with a hangover.

Forever afterwards Lorenzo turned up his beak at fancy wines regardless of occasion. He even declined food items on his smorgasbord tray in the outdoor cage if any wine had been used in their preparation— except lobster Newburg: his abstinence did not include absurdity.

Shortly before maturity his appetite tapered off to a point where he rarely ate more than a quarter of his weight in food each day. Minced earthworm *à la nature* ranked low on his savor list—about D-. Offered *spaghetti al pomodoro,* he beamed with an expression almost anyone could read: "I should work so hard to pull the same things out of the ground . . . minus the *pomodoro?*" When we really wished to impress him, we included broccoli Hollandaise, rice pilaf, Boston strawberries, and cake dough. He "raved" in his own native dialect, so we never really knew what he "said" about dry bread he could dunk in honey-sweetened goat's milk.

Indoors Lorenzo never failed to invite himself to our meals. His table manners were like his other manners: barbaric. Without so much as a hint of permission, he hogged food from our plates, forks, spoons, cups, glasses—and mouths. Weeks after Lea had begun placing a daily vitamin pill near my plate, we discovered that Lorenzo—always first to answer the dinner bell, first to arrive at the table—had surreptitiously swallowed each vitamin dose without one later burp, which made me question the value of my high-priced placebos. On the other hand, the super pepper-uppers may have accounted at least in part for his behavior and appetite.

A neighbor across the street came by at breakfast time one day to borrow a cup of sugar. Mrs. Ex is proper to her fingertips, and as the recipient of earlier jaybird sass, she was barely on speaking terms with Lorenzo. Each recognized in the other an accessible definition of the verb *dislike*. Ignoring her existence that morning, Lorenzo perched—of all places—on the rim of the sugar bowl, where he indulged his sweet tooth. Mrs. Ex was mortified to learn that we allowed "that unsanitary scalawag" on the table.

"Goodness!" she exclaimed. "Does that creature get into the sugar?"

Lea, being Swiss, is undiplomatically truthful. Sometimes I could wring her neck for it.

"Oh, yes, Mrs. Ex. This morning Lorenzo is a bit exasperating. He's been into everything. He sipped some of Bob's orange juice, but he's very careful when he perches on a glass and sips. He had fried bacon and egg that he got from Bob's fork. When he sits on the sugar bowl like that, he is really signaling Bob to use more sugar. Lorenzo has always taken Bob's coffee sweet—with cream."

"He has his own dish," I added, trying to regain some respectability.

Lea continued to lead with her chin. "Yes, but he'd rather eat from ours. I might say, he's perfectly clean. He never steps in his own droppings, but you should see him wade across a bowl of oatmeal. Jays may be clean, but they are the sloppiest eaters."

"Unless it's bad weather, he has lunch and supper outside in his coop," I said quickly.

"What does he eat besides breakfast?" I'm sure Mrs. Ex thought birds were like statues, dry on the inside.

"Smorgasbord," I said. "He eats according to his mood of the moment."

"He's really hooked on slushy dishes—apple sauce, prune whip, apricot puree," Lea went on. "But afterwards it's disastrous for the sofa—I mean when he fills up on elderberries or blueberries."

Mrs. Ex borrowed less after that. I was sorry, because we rather needed her to keep us more conventional. I don't say that Lea was following a plan. It just sounded that way.

Aside from Mrs. Ex, there were several living beings that Lorenzo found it hard to put up with—probably due to another facet of his personality: he suffered jealous tantrums. If a dog, another bird, or in some cases people, occupied our attention for more than a short time, the jay made his jealousy known by standing on one of our shoulders, shifting from foot to foot, and shrieking. More often than not, he power-dived any bird or mammal that came near. As punishment for dealing with other creatures, we received hammerhead pecks to the back of the neck and gravelly "mad talk" immediately after a visitor's exit. Much later when he had our undivided attention, Lorenzo forgave with dramatic neck cuddles, "love talk," and the soft-eye (half-lidded). He was pathologically jealous.

Lorenzo took every possible step toward violating our privacy. If I tried to type in my study of an evening or if Lea was occupied in another part of the house for more than five minutes, the jay would seek out the missing member. Habitually he landed scrappily on a shoulder and pecked or "howled" until the three of us were reunited. He couldn't have cared less whether we spent our time in the den or some other room as long as we were all together, but we think he preferred the den and the living room because he rarely hid portable objects except in those rooms.

Getting back to breach of privacy, if either of us lingered too long over a bathroom magazine, we surely heard a none-too-gentle tapping at the bottom of the door, accompanied by a now-familiar "running-water gurgle." When Lorenzo's idea of polite rapping failed to bring us out, he flew to the doorknob and gave the woodwork numerous reasons for refinishing. It reminded us of red-headed woodpeckers at an old-time woodpecking contest.

Everyone who has attended an old-time woodpecking contest in some local " 'Possum Hollow" will know exactly what I mean.

In addition to monopolizing the spotlight and banging on closed doors, our jay developed a certain personal recklessness. We believe he risked his neck in original stunts to get the attention he craved. Like the notorious sixteenth-century Spanish rogue, Lazarillo de Tormes, Lorenzo may have been born to amuse: first himself, then others. Reasons behind Lazarillo's wayward deeds were food, lodging, and larceny . . . with detours into attention-getting devilment for devilment's sake. Lorenzo scored heavily on originality of motives. I never looked into his tricky eyes without considering the possibility that he might have been Lazarillo reincarnated, given that both were incurably set against growing up. Probably looking to people as his model, Lorenzo never behaved better than he had to at any time.

When Lea puttered around the flower beds, she wore a straw hat with a wide brim covered with ridiculous bright-colored Hong Kong plastic blossoms. Lorenzo apparently felt that flowers belonged on soil-rooted plants. When Lea set the hat aside one day in the patio, he decided not only to "plant" those flowers in *our* garden but also to be sure the neighbors got their share. He flew from yard to yard, "setting out" synthetic geraniums, fake petunias, counterfeit orchids, and bogus nasturtiums. Of course, he didn't really set them out; he scattered the flossy flowers from hell to breakfast as if he were working for the west wind.

When the jay failed to return after carrying away the last "blossom," we organized a search party. He refused to answer when we called his name and whistled. We trudged up and down the block, searching unfriendly properties, reasonably certain that he was not about to move out on us. I looked for blue feathers every time a cat scampered from a bush. At last we spotted six wild jays hovering and squawking in the shrubbery five properties south of ours. Rushing into the yard, ignoring a vicious German shepherd, we found Lorenzo unconscious under an oleander bush. He was limp . . . looked dead when I picked him up.

His eyes were closed; his mouth hung half-open at one end of a limp neck.

We know a veterinarian, five miles away in North Hollywood, who seems indifferent to people and loves animals. The good doctor specializes in the treatment of birds, and he claims he engages them in meaningful dialogue.

Lea wrapped our bird like a mummy and laid him in a padded shoebox. We sped to the veterinary clinic, where the vet placed Lorenzo on a stainless steel operating table and covered him with a clear plastic tent while an attendant turned on the oxygen. Lea and I hugged a corner in total silence. The vet stroked his chin (his own, not Lorenzo's . . . Lorenzo didn't need a chin).

There was no sign of breathing, and it looked as though our jay wouldn't make it.

"I suppose we'll bury him under the Abyssinian delphiniums," I suggested in a whisper.

"No," Lea disagreed, shaking her head slowly. She is more sentimental than I am. "Let's bury him under something he liked—the Jerusalem artichokes. Hey, look! He's opening an eye!"

Slowly the second eye came to life. Lorenzo focused on me with murder in his expression. Deliberately and excitedly, he crawled to his feet, skidding around on the slick table. When he regained his sense of balance, he ran around inside the tent, pecking at every angle for an opening. The attendant carefully removed the cover. Lorenzo flew to the vet's shoulder, yakked bloody murder, and tried his best to remove the man's earlobe.

Indestructible Lorenzo! His encounter was another form of self-determination. The Lazarillo complex.

"That'll be five dollars," said the vet. "Three for the oxygen. Two for the pecked earlobe. You want an itemized bill?"

Lea was concentrating on the fact that the bird was on an oxygen high. "Oh, no," she said absently, "don't do anything to his bill! We'll take care of that."

"Just so you take care of mine," said the vet.

We never learned what Lorenzo had done to end up under the oleander, but we gave the jaybird assembly benefit of all doubt so far as their reasons for ganging up on him were concerned. It was his habit to sass, back talk, and puff out his feathers every time another jay flew onto our property. Puffed out feathers meant, "You bum, I could knock your block off!" So I'd hazard a guess they probably seized the opportunity to get back at him as he flitted about distributing Lea's Hong Kong plastics—out of range of my rock-throwing arm. Maybe the other jays tried to teach him the outdoors manners his home influence had failed to instill.

7

EVEN ON THE OCCASION OF HIS VISIT
to the vet, the intensity and exactness of Lorenzo's
ability to communicate impressed human observers.
The changing look in his eye clearly revealed curiosity, in-depth study, likes and dislikes, enthusiasm, feelings of abuse, resentment, restless boredom, and once
in a while, downright hatred. These were the everyday
expressions he made known. No one ever accused
Lorenzo of being poker-faced or single-pointed. His
protruding eyes could look the other way and catch
us when we tried to hide something from him.

Though he was often slippery, Lorenzo forced us to be honest with him.

His sweeping, high-arched white eyebrow feathers grew in only as the jay reached maturity. White eyebrows accentuated the intensity of all his facial expressions. When we ignored an especially strong signal—aimed to demand attention—we received a pencil, thimble, or small spoon accurately bombsighted to the tops of our heads, particularly if Lorenzo got the idea we were deliberately ignoring him. We made absolutely no assignment of human traits to this bird. Nevertheless, there were specific areas in Lorenzo's makeup that raised questions: those wise looks that appeared to betoken specific meanings, glances insinuating that punishment for a committed misdemeanor had been justified, and sounds in combination with movements—signals presumably to communicate an important specific message, punishment, or love—these made you stop and think.

When you live long enough with another creature, you develop an understanding of signals that accompany movements, sounds, and glances. As a result of our limited experience, Lea and I decided that the bird or mammal gets to know a lot more about the person because it spends more time studying the two-legger than vice versa; a dog or cat knows more about its human patron than man could possibly know about the pet. For years Lois Crisler gathered evidence of intelligent "eye talk" from her extensive studies of Alaska timber wolves in deep wilderness. According to Crisler, simple communication between man and animals gets short-circuited because man has either lost or deliberately steeled himself against what the *animal enthusiasts* call messages. We are congenitally inclined to downgrade nonhuman ability to think, given that ancient teachings denied mental and emotional processes beyond instinct to "lower" animals. Those who hesitate to accept communication between man and beast have never owned a dog . . . not to mention a bear cub . . . or a jaybird. Doubters should read J. Allen Boone's *Kinship with All Life.* Boone was a friend of ours for many years, during which time we watched him convey optical messages to a dog that performed numerous tasks in response to Boone's "eye talk." Not a repertoire, but unrelated tasks.

When "dialogue" between Lorenzo and a person

succeeded, it was the result of endless effort upon the bird's part and some human effort. I credit the jay with at least ninety percent of the struggle, because the bird worked harder and longer than people to impart an "idea." Invariably he began his announcement of each bulletin in low key, but unless his meaning registered right away, he broke out everything at his command to put a notion across, including physical violence if that was what it took. During the breakdown of his early wildland fears and barriers, he must have sensed our gentle and sincere intentions but clumsy ignorance when it came to blue jays. In his own way—if impatient and prone to use shortcuts at times—Lorenzo gave us a clear-cut picture of animal needs beyond basic food and shelter. One of those important needs, we discovered, was expressing love for another creature. His trust and need for togetherness expressed his love for Lea and me. He may have been crude and demanding, but no animal we ever knew could express greater love with more subtlety than Lorenzo. He had all sorts of expressions, sounds, and movements that proclaimed honest-to-goodness, unmistakable love.

After recognizing that he could make us understand most of his whims—including his honest love for us—Lorenzo seemed to steer our lives around to more and more complicated commands. At times he was plainly exasperating until we became

more fluent in understanding his increasingly sophisticated idiom. For example, during evening romps, he
dropped thimbles, peanuts, pencils, staple removers,
and clothespins into places from which he knew he
could never recover them by himself. He reminded us
of his distant cousin in Mark Twain's story *What
Stumped the Blue Jays.*

Of course, Mark Twain was writing fiction and he
carried the idea a lot further than modern scientific
thought would accept, but there is a thread of truth
throughout the story. He claimed that jays enjoyed
"showing off" and did so by "talking." From what we
gathered from Lorenzo, we go along with that. Twain
said, "There's more to a blue jay than any other creature." We don't buy that. But the great humorist
further asserted that the jay has more moods and feelings than other creatures and that ". . . bird is capable
of putting it all into language . . . bristling with
metaphor . . . seldom using bad grammar." He tried
to prove the point that "A jay hasn't got any more
principle than a Congressman." Twain's allegory of
the jay trying to fill the bottomless hole with acorns
reminded everyone of the futility of hard labor against
an impossible task.

Twain should have known Lorenzo. We often
thought our quixotic jay lived exclusively by the principle of the "impossible dream."

So when Lorenzo "lost" something behind the sofa

and yelled until we recovered it for him, we were careful not to allow that little game to go too far. His nightly repetition of these performances all but drove us up the wall. He rarely seemed to tire. His act of purposely dropping something into an impossible place had little to do with the article per se. He had hatched a creative idea to bring one or both of us into his activity.

In a crowded field of backyard performers, Lorenzo required but six months to become outstanding. We often watched from a distance through binoculars while he played deeply serious games by himself. One of his solitaires in his outdoor coop involved moving, lining up, and moving again a collection of unshelled nuts. Given that jays kick around a whole world of symbols, this nut-moving may have symbolized his future habit of burying nuts, then trying to relocate them later. He often moved his cache of outdoor toys from beneath one pile of shredded newspaper to the bottom of another pile. This was not simple random hiding of material possessions. For the most part, the orderly arrangement of toys under the second crumpled mound of paper was very much like the first. Metal washers that he could carry in his beak caused him to jump, roll, run, and fly around the big coop. I suggest that the principle of the circle may have impressed him differently than did his other odd-shaped toys.

On the lawn he enticed other blue jays, Kaufman, or both to seize an aluminum ring and fly around with it in their beaks, chased by other noisy participants until the ring was dropped. At this point another bird would swoop down, yelling his lungs out, grab the ring, and fly away with it until he or she dropped it. From our point of view, the game had a distinct drawback: the jays and Kaufman didn't confine themselves to our backyard. They frequently flew away and lost the attractive toy. Replacement rings weren't exactly inexpensive, and we never knew a ring to return later. Thus, science was deprived of further earth-shaking knowledge because of a low budget. One possible evolutionary drawback to these games stumped us for a spell: Kaufman imitated shrieking jays so often that we feared he might lose his own native raucous squawk. He never did.

Lorenzo's games with people demanded plotting and understanding for delight value. His early promotion of hide-and-seek never ceased to captivate his attention; he played the game with increasing skill for as long as he was with us. His little game of trading a lesser item for an article of jewelry was uncanny. Yet he certainly recognized the vast differences between games with his fellow wildlings and his pastime activities with people. Thus, with his peers he never engaged in deliberate "loss" of items or in hide-and-seek as he did with human competitors. And we never saw genuine evidence of his "horse-trading" ability among his fellow birds.

Long on beak and short on tact when deprived of jewelry, scissors, matches, razor blades, or evening monkeyshines that he had planned ahead of time, Lorenzo pitched tantrums far more effective than his playacting in games. "Talkathons" and cocky swaggers across the human lap were frequent. He had no fear of his foster parents. Wing slaps across the nose bridge followed pretended injury to a wing or leg that went unnoticed, as well as occasional regurgitation, and defecation as often as gut refills permitted. If he was still unsuccessful in getting his way, he crouched on my chest or clung to my goatee with both feet and seized a lip with a bloodletting peck.

I was bawling him out one night for that very deed when he reached into my mouth and grabbed my tongue. I clamped down on his recently straightened beak and bit it just hard enough for him to get the picture.

Shrieking at the top of his vocal cords while backing down to my lap to take stock of his predicament, he stood for a moment and quivered with a combination of surprise and rage. He shook his head and whetted his beak on my jeans for a fresh attack. Instead of flying into my face with a score to settle as I expected him to do, however, he locked his talons in my curly goatee, fluttered his wings, and "sobbed" for almost two minutes. He kept his gaze locked with mine throughout the adventure.

Prompted by a noisy conscience, I was about to offer him a shiny new penny when he reached for my wounded lip, nibbled it ever so gently, and "soft-talked." Although he picked our teeth, tweaked our noses and earlobes, and nibbled our lips often, he never again dealt a hammerhead blow to any part of any human face to my knowledge.

Thus, we communicated in two ways: he knew exactly how to demand what he wanted, and he knew exactly how to help me hate myself for the only time I ever punished him.

Recognizing our frequent failures to interpret nuances that were meaningful to him, we tried first to understand each of Lorenzo's general areas of communication, followed by specific possibilities of meaning. We also appreciated the fact that a nonlinguistic animal had to translate *all* abstracts into physical symbols before they could be interpreted by human computer. Light nibbling in contrast to hammerhead blows meant "I'm sorry." Mild vocal utterances barely above a whisper or ranging all the way to full-scale shrieks meant "Please give me that!" depending upon what he wanted and how badly. We believe the *please* was most often omitted. The hop, the swagger, the walk, the crawl were nuances of "I'm ready to play now; how about you?"

We resent those sentimentalists who maintain that animals other than *Homo sapiens* speak or even think in any kind of semantic language of their own. They don't! On the other hand, we hesitate to accept the dictum that bird sounds and movements merely proclaim territorial imperatives. Conveyance of thought among birds is far more complicated as an evolved system than that. Among our records of most birds we have cared for and released, there is ample documentation of rudimentary abstract thinking. For more obvious examples, consider the signals and voice commands of leader geese and ducks, and the oral sentry-to-sentry "reports" around the perimeter of grackle, starling, and blackbird flocks. You have seen these flights of a hundred or more birds leave a feast and hit the air instantly at one vocal signal—or the single flick of a wing. Even though every bird seemed to be talking at the same time, apparently there was always an eye on the Alpha.

Masters of turmoil with an eye on order, blue jays drop what they are doing to issue their notorious "Yank! Yank! Yank!" warning of a hunter's approach in the wilds. In Canada I've entertained whiskey jacks (jay cousins) in camp. These jaylike birds use a variety of "vocabulary" and the "yo-yo complex" (jumping up and down like monkeys, raccoons, and bear cubs) to elicit handouts.

It should be added that when all other sounds and gestures failed, Lorenzo made his point in song . . . provided he considered an issue important enough for the creation of a genuine three-alarm disturbance. Outdoors he often called—shrieked—from his coop, but when he sang a beautiful harmonious "tune," I always rushed to his side to find out what was up. Most times I had to evict a gopher snake, chunk a cat over the fence, scare off a hawk, shoot a weasel, or confiscate some kid's BB gun.

When the chords of Beethoven, Brahms, or Bach swelled from the stereo, Lorenzo yielded temporarily and shut up. Invariably he relinquished his own "program" with grace when classical music was played. By contrast, most canned ballads of Joan Baez caused him to accompany the music from lampshade, curtain rod, or human hat. He issued breezy, jumbled sounds—

completely unjaylike "dialect"—when he fidgeted with new harmony. Once I plucked him from the air during an Elvis Presley rehash. He acted as if he had taken leave of his sanity. As I held him finally on his back, he continued a crazy, off-key accompaniment all the way to the rattly end of the rock-and-roll number. We learned to be extremely selective about what we allowed to emerge from the stereo.

Like linnets and mockingbirds, Lorenzo could "sing," "wolfwhistle," or just yell while wingborne, perched, or handheld. People can't sing too well upside down, but Lorenzo *could* and *did*.

After concealing a microphone behind a patio planter in order to eavesdrop on his continuing affair with an older neighborhood jayhen, we taped his slickest vanity in "song" and "talk." He would have been fiercely hassled had this come to his attention, but we had to be prepared—so we rationalized—since this particular jayhen's mate was the Alpha jaycock who tolerated no nonsense from any other local jay.

Several other cassette tapes revealed that Lorenzo also changed his vocal "expression" to suit times of day, night, occasion, or audience, just as mockingbirds, cuckoos, and nightingales do. It was his voice that aroused the feathered tenants of Fig Leaf Towers on the opposite side of the lawn some thirty feet from the chicken-wire coop where he matured. Quiet and peaceful species that had nested there for a dozen years —seldom seen or heard during brooding—became loud, belligerent, and "show-offy" as the result of Lorenzo's vocal needling. The jay's incessant and intentional disturbances almost made us go as far as Mark Twain in attributing semantic gobbledygook to him: a linguistic idiom that incited scrappy behavior between nests in the Towers.

One sultry August afternoon Lorenzo apparently tempted several neighborhood jays to land on his coop and engage in a singalong. High-pitched shrieks and cries split the air, rendering impossible the relaxed billet of incubation going on in the Towers.

When towhees, mockingbirds, thrashers, juncos, linnets, and white crowns gathered on the sidelines and silently watched, the jays got the message, broke up their festival, and left. I've heard comedians in the San Fernando Valley say they get the squeamishes from *silent* audiences. Similarly, jays hunger for applause, the more the better. An icy camera stare is easily misinterpreted—even in jayland, I suppose.

Our jay—I say *our,* but nobody really owns a jay —anyway, our jay may have exerted his most disturbing influences on the so-called silent ground dwellers: towhees, thrushes, thrashers, quail. During Lorenzo's maturation, these normally hushed visitors popped into the yard and shrieked like fighting tomcats.

8

THAT WAS NOT THE LAST WORD ON the subject of hubbub. Lorenzo created indoor disturbances in addition to his long list of backyard commotions. One such detour into the world of the ridiculous involved mirrors. Since boyhood I have raised dozens of birds belonging to at least two dozen different genera, ranging from hummingbirds to eagles. I recall but eight individuals who paid any attention to "that other bird" in the mirror. Besides Lorenzo, robins, hawks, and magpies were the only birds I have known that either pecked, footed, or "made friends" with the twin they could never quite touch. Eagles went bananas.

Magazine reports often state that birds recognize themselves in a mirror. We don't deny that possibility. We simply question it until more proof is forthcoming. Considering the hiss, squawk, or peck aimed at his reflection when he passed a mirror, Lorenzo apparently did not recognize himself. In order to overdo his challenge, however, he ruffled his plumage and throttled down his voice to a destructive undertone exactly the way he did when he met other jays outdoors. So, by seeing a jay in the looking glass, he developed supple feather-erecting muscles for instant shock value or display effect. But so did that "other jay." Lorenzo, then looking the other way, executed several artificial struts past the mirror with hawkish side-glances.

A jay's jayness allows him to shuffle resources in order to win temporary battles today. Who cares about tomorrow?

With puzzling exceptions during those rugged months of growing up, Lorenzo's dealings with backyard neighbors, peers, confreres, and mismatches corroborated few theories of peaceful togetherness. Total rout was the general rule. His generosity toward the mother red squirrel had to be an exception; he fed her repeatedly. But whenever a cockerel jay landed on his cage, Lorenzo gobbled every bite of food his crop could hold rather than offering to share any. Then he vomited from overeating—every time. He would have put a pig to shame.

Once an escaped parakeet—a ragged and hungry little wanderer—came to the cage and begged a hand-out from the overflowing smorgasbord. While pacing an arrogant strut back and forth, Lorenzo sang what we called his "I-loathe-a-bum" song. He then stepped over to his chopped spinach, the food he liked the least (although he yelled his head off if we omitted it). He placed a small beakful in the open doorway, just inside the cage. I reemphasize that his door was as a rule open . . . closed only when he was "in protective custody." When the parakeet reached inside for the meager bite, Lorenzo dealt his meanest hammerhead thrust to the top of his victim's head.

The closest Lorenzo ever came to a civilized relationship was with an old friend of ours, a durable screech owl we called Olie, who lived in a tall syca-more on Fulton Avenue, half a block west. The property *butted* ours in the rear (to quote local legalese).

We had raised Olie from a two-eyed cotton ball that someone had left on our porch about ten years before. Not only did the diminutive owl decline to leave the neighborhood upon release, but also as far as we were able to determine, he quashed all romantic advances made by owlhens. Olie was a born misogynist. We saw him beat the daylights out of more than one screechhen. Clearly no good ever came of the vitamins, minerals, and enzymes we tendered. He ate them all, including raw oysters!

I don't believe we overdid the recommended diced mice laced with male hormone.

Don't tell me that owls are loaded with smart! Compared with a blue jay, an owl's IQ wouldn't even reach comfortable room temperature . . . about 70.

We never knew how or when Lorenzo began his visits to Olie's "door," and although our ears did a slow burn now and then, we knew even less what owl and jay may have "discussed." We did, however, feel reasonably sure that the strange relationship—in dramatic contrast with Lorenzo's dealings with most neighborhood creatures—was friendly in an astringently formal way. Through binoculars we often watched Olie step sedately from his knot-hole doorway where he seemed to stand most of the time even when rain blew in on his face. During Lorenzo's visits, the owl sat on a limb within a foot of the jay, but the birds were too far away either to photograph or to tape their mumbo jumbo. "Conversation" may have become heated on occasion, because we have seen both beaks moving rapidly at the same time, as well as pointed wing slaps directed against branches. Olie was born with a frown on his face to go with a congenital

grouch. For a while after each visit, the jay would perch on a dowel in his pen, where he appeared to engage in deep meditation. From time to time he would issue soft, pipy notes to add to the mystery.

According to one diary entry, Olie was indisposed one summer afternoon, so Lorenzo spent his time eyeing a flock of crows that spiraled skyward on thermal updrafts. The jay seemed game to try the same maneuver, but when I released him he soon discovered that his saucer-shaped wings had not been designed to take advantage of sun-heated shafts of air. I may have snickered at his efforts, because when he returned to earth he flew to the garage roof, wagged his tail in a circle, and "snarled" through his mustache while staring straight into my eyes.

"What's the matter with Lorenzo?" Lea called from the patio door.

"Skip it," I said. "We are both jousting the blades of the same mill. Lazarillo de Tormes has just thrown Don Quixote."

In addition to extravagances with song, food, and a desire to soar, Lorenzo grew up loving the light of day. How brightly his plumage reflected sunshine in the flash of his shiny blue wings as he scudded up and down the neighborhood, ostensibly bargaining for trouble, scandal, or ripe fruit at every tree and shrub. Like sunshine, a jaybird's radiant self dims only when something comes between him and his perennial pursuit of lightheartedness—from the top of a telephone pole to the bottom of a farkleberry bush.

One morning while caged behind a locked door because of some infraction, Lorenzo squawked for release. Ordinarily we turned him loose when he insisted because he always returned shortly after flying some errand of critical importance. But on that morning I saw his pledged enemy, the big bully Alpha jay —mate of the jayhen for whom Lorenzo sometimes composed and warbled dazzling arias. I suspected our little fool was on a collision course with disaster. The big jay, who carried a grudge for every male jay in the vicinity, sat riding out the zephyrs on a telephone cable at the back of the property. From there he glared down at Lorenzo and me.

Deciding to play along, I released Lorenzo. Our jay flew a beeline for the cable where the veteran stood up, ready to demonstrate what bird students call "territorial integrity," in this instance, *territorial machismo*. Lorenzo's flight and tinny war cry must have broadcasted an immediate alert to the local bird population. Nary a movement in the trees; no bird cheeped, but they all ogled as the two gladiators prepared for battle. As I appraised the way Lorenzo braked his flight just before colliding with the big jay, I thought perhaps our bird might have cursed his rashness and changed his mind.

As "all fleas have little fleas upon their backs to bite 'em," every creature has another being to fear. How on earth did pampered, crippled, undersized Lorenzo hope to evict a seasoned antagonist almost twice his gross? Most jaybird survival, we have unscientifically concluded from homespun documentation, depends upon the ability to bluster and bluff.

With plumage hackled to enhance the bigger and tougher look, Lorenzo lowered his head and charged. The old jay barely moved to duck the young bird's poor marksmanship. Lorenzo braked, turned, and streamlined his equipment for divebombing. Allied with gravity during the downward thrust, he learned a valuable strategic maneuver: never charge an enemy blue jay from a vertical course. If you do, the unprincipled foe will dodge your thrust at the last fraction of a second, then sledgehammer the back of your head as you are borne earthward by your fickle ally, gravity.

When Lorenzo barreled within range, the big jay perpetrated the final insult: he looped the loop as he rabbit-punched our hero with a feather-showering blow. Returning to the utility cable, he watched Lorenzo—wings fully spread—spiral to earth like a miniature helicopter that had just run out of fuel. The flight was over before I could root for the underdog.

Lorenzo was out cold when I caught him.

Tossing him onto the floor of his cage, I ran for an

ice cube to stem the flow of blood at the back of his head. When I returned he was staggering and muttering from one corner of his aviary to another like a pugilist demanding a return match. In his own jaybird world he must have discovered that hope is neither victory nor any fraction thereof.

The big jay leered down at me. If I had owned a shotgun. . . .

By nightfall the decisive battle was history in the community, and Lorenzo's mettlesome curiosity was again full steam ahead. As a fledgling, he had probed with beak and talons every surface and article he could contact. His most tingling curiosity at all times, however, concerned the human body. Of an evening, he worked from toes to knees to Adam's apple to ears and to mouth. Then he dropped back to hands, where he carefully tested each finger, ring, and wristwatch.

Indoors or out, he landed on the human shoulder to present petitions to ears . . . whispered if begged, screamed if involved in complaint. Lorenzo never hinted. Somehow and at some secret time, he learned that ears were the receptors of sound. He was extremely curious about faces and rarely devoted less than half an hour to explore a single beard, mustache, or protruding hair from ear or nostril. He checked out the several skin textures of our guests—lips, noses, cheeks, chins—but never touched an eye. A favorite probe was teeth. He tapped lightly on each front tooth, used rougher tactics on gold crowns until he learned they would not yield. We warned guests with removable bridges.

You don't get too many guests with removable bridges who allow a blue jay to peck around inside their mouths. Not more than once anyway.

To Lorenzo, tongues were huge, thick worms that poked out at him . . . once. Naked toes were tough old bugs spoiling for a fight. Because that was where he accrued early knowledge in the field of calisthenics, he never outgrew a warlike attitude toward naked toes, but he demanded real bug wiggling for stalking practice. It was during his ongoing micro-war against toes that might be in some way associated with elastic gear that we produced, to our knowledge, the only "growling" or "snarling" bird.

I don't believe that even Mark Twain ever bragged about knowing a bird that *growled*.

One night a woman wearing a wig came to see Lorenzo. By that time the unusual jay was attracting public attention due to some feature stories about him. The lady's neat little hairpiece, anchored to her own curls by two bobby pins, ignited instant curiosity in the jay because the wig's coltish color was meant to contrast rather than blend with natural hair. That made no sense to Lorenzo, who instantly attacked the problem in his usual way. The intrepid woman thought it was cute and uncommon to have a blue jay wade around in her hair. She should have read somebody's immortal poem:

> I think that I shall never wear
> A nest of blue jays in my hair!

All humor ceased, however, after that sneaky creep secretly removed the two bobby pins, seized the wig between his mandibles, flew to the fireplace, and stuffed the expensive hairpiece into the ashes before anyone could thwart his plan.

For Lea and me the worst part was that ever afterwards Lorenzo believed every woman's scalp should yield a wig when he pulled . . . and pull he could!

Ordinarily gentle with our regular guests as well as strangers who dropped in to see "that phenomenon," Lorenzo took unfair advantage during a heat wave and received a D- in deportment for the entire month. For his just deserts he remained locked up in his cage most of that time. He became so mischievous we had to supply people with toys he had never seen before so they could bribe him away from jewelry, keys, buttons, pins, brooches, money, and hair. We warned women against opening a handbag in his presence. He could lightfinger a clutch purse and ditch the contents with a professional purse-snatcher's skill in nothing flat. One guest of a certain age who failed to heed our warning was emotionally upset when that obstreperous bird knocked her open handbag from a table, ransacked the contents, then flew about the house with her driver's license that revealed her birthdate.

Lorenzo may not have been afraid to reveal the contents of a woman's purse—or what lay under her wig—but he looked upon passing aircraft as the most terrorizing of experiences. Every time he

saw or heard an approaching airplane he crawled under whatever was near and gargled. Our home lay directly in line with the Van Nuys Airport flight pattern, so I had to build the jay several air-raid shelters for his peace of mind, especially when show-offs in low-flying planes swooped overhead. His shelters were in the form of small birdhouses spaced around the front and rear gardens. Unfortunately, squatter sparrows, finches, and towhees were soon hatching nestlings in the attractive shelters, so the jay had to learn to scurry under the house when air traffic terrorized him. But his curiosity soon got the best of him, and he popped out for a quick look before the aircraft disappeared.

9

To keep Lorenzo's curiosity and alertness primed, we often introduced new objects into the den where we spent most evenings with him: a new clock, a bowl of nuts, knickknacks, bric-a-brac, pictures. He raised no ruckus when we removed a regular fixture, but showed immediate fascination toward any "extra." At once he inspected different shoes, shirt, blouse, socks, jewelry. I threw him for a loop one night by wearing a tennis shoe on one foot and a loafer on the other. I never did that again. The jay "howled" at such a pitch that one nosey neighbor called and asked if I was "plucking Lorenzo's feathers." We believe he was the one who called the SPCA earlier because he thought the jay's loud yelling indicated abuse. He was the man who pretended to despise all blue jays as a class.

Out-of-doors, Lorenzo's first reaction to strange shoes was to untie the laces. The first time I sported my western hat, he pecked a hole in it before I could protect it. If you really wanted to shake him out of a tree, all you had to do was wear a bright-yellow necktie on a red shirt. Notorious for his own bad taste, Lorenzo apparently had no tolerance for the violations of others, at least so far as sartorial decorum was concerned.

Of an evening when he first came into the den, he instantly spotted any furniture shift, rearrangement, or addition. As if snooping into our private lives, one of his first evening projects was to empty the wastebaskets and redistribute the contents about the house: under rugs, behind shelved books, even under bedroom pillows. I shall not go into the abominations he committed in our bathrooms except to say that I rarely took a bath when Lorenzo didn't sit on top of the shower door and sing to the flow of water.

His principal project of an evening was looting. Pencils, paperclips, and ballpoints he never bothered to steal with class. Those he just took. But not with the obvious gusto with which he lifted small tools, loose money, or recent snapshots. Stealing was a craft he employed as an art. After all, he was only practicing indoors what was for real up and down the community. We have observed many picaresque life styles among wildlings—and several humans—but Lorenzo took the cake.

We often associated this bird's curiosity and klepto-mania with his keen eyesight. Jays are slightly popeyed. Someone called the dark, mellow color of their eyes "soot with sparkles." Lorenzo's eyes appeared exaggerated because highly arched white "eye-brow" feathers stood out against his blue head, always lending a brow-lifted look of amazement. A false impression. Nothing, *but nothing,* amazed that bird.

Ornithologists assert that the jay's field of vision covers 320 degrees. We don't contest the erudition. We simply argue that Lorenzo's field of vision covered everybody else's property: instead of eyesight degrees, he had a larceny coefficient.

Because of his superb eyesight he could explore on the wing any room or yard without ever flying into windowpanes or mirrors as other birds did. In poor light we have seen him dart seventy feet to catch a caterpillar that was feasting on a leaf's *under* side. And his vision was only average when you consider that raptors can recognize a mouse's characteristic movements a quarter mile away.

Besides the gift of reasonably normal eyesight,

Lorenzo was also endowed with an impressive sense of touch. He used to probe with his beak (and got away with it) the many animals he met—dogs, squirrels, lizards, mice, and other birds. To prove his sophisticated sense of choice, he was careful not to probe any cats, snakes, or hawks. One morning he had been free-flying for an hour without visual or auditory evidence of having toppled the neighborhood wildlife while he was on the loose. As it happened, a man of untidy habits up the block had at long last noticed mice droppings on his patio. Since local squirrel-fed owls snubbed such measly tidbits as lowly mice—and Olie could handle but one a day—the man had finally set out an old-fashioned mousetrap. On that very day we heard an unfamiliar clatter at our back door accompanied by Lorenzo's muffled wheeze. Rushing out, we found the jay "cursing" through his nostrils. The mousetrap was securely attached to his beak.

When I freed him he flew into the elm for several minutes, where he let off a head of steam and then glided down to the planter where I had thrown the trap. After brazenly eating the cheese bait off the trigger, Lorenzo gave the device a sound thrashing with beak and talons. For once he didn't blame me for his misadventure.

When I approached our neighbor, he reluctantly agreed to set all traps out of bird reach. He called later and admitted that he had seen a blue jay catch, kill, and devour a young mouse.

After Lorenzo had weathered neighborhood hazards, daily guests, and room changes—along with other unusual distractions bound to happen around the "Loonybin"—he settled down to simple daily routines, uncomplicated little pleasures, and light "chatter." During such sessions, he climbed to my chest and combed my beard for half an hour, first with beak, later with talons. Then he loved to chase my pen across the pages of his story. We think he nibbled the ballpoint pen because it recalled those chickhood eye-dropper days of soups, fruit juices, and honeyed goat's milk. After fussing with the pen, he often went to his toy chest, brought me the old eyedropper, then followed me to the refrigerator where I took out a favorite liquid. He stood wide-legged like a fledgling while I delivered the goody into his open mouth, but

since he got all the milk and juices he wanted in his outdoor cage, this eyedropper rigmarole may have been jay-constituted nostalgia. I hasten to say that we rejected a neighbor's explanation that "Lorenzo tried to recall the past."

After the eyedropper course of procedure, the jay often spent part of an evening on the sofa back and sang softly while he undid Lea's hair curlers or tweaked her earlobes when jewelry wouldn't "give." We found those curlers in the most uncustomary places, especially if someone had forgotten to put down the toilet seat or close the door to the flour bin.

As he was shuttling back and forth across my chest one Saturday afternoon while I was taking the first sunbath of summer, Lorenzo began to emit pipsqueaky notes and drawn-out lisps that I had never heard before. He was not yet a full year old, but he was thoroughly capable of communicating his message. Like every other blue jay I've ever heard of or read about, he considered people his intellectual inferiors. I may be accused of fiction, but it took no deep knowledge of ornithology to recognize moods and attitudes in this bird. On that June afternoon he enjoyed an excitement and wished to share it with me, somewhat as he had done on numerous previous occasions. As a rule, his body movements and facial expressions repeated what went on in his head. At times it was as simple as that.

One eminent bird person contested our statements concerning a bird's ability to cast facial expressions until she met Lorenzo. He did upset so many well-rutted wagonwheels.

After a dozen vocal outbursts—followed by tugs of war with the hair on my chest—the jay succeeded in leading me to the service yard near the rear property line. He ushered me straight to a fence corner where he dropped to the ground and skipped back and forth like a football player who has just outrun the field for a touchdown. His eyes fairly jumped out at me as he leaned back and "hollered."

A nestling linnet, probably a dropout from Fig Leaf Towers, lay on the ground, gasping for breath. A mother linnet flitted about, demonstrating her emotional devastation and helplessness. I was instantly conscious of eyes staring from every leafy plane in the surrounding yards. There was an unnatural silence throughout the steamy community. I stooped down and picked up the naked nestling. How did Lorenzo know the little bird was on the ground? The jay sang his loudest "victory song" as he rode my shoulder to the house. He balanced on my wrist and gabbled while Lea and I watered the chick with the jay's old eyedropper.

Many the knowing look (and sassy facial expression) shot my way the rest of that Saturday afternoon. And if it is true—and I've lots of evidence that it is —that the eye is the window opening upon the animal soul, the jay's gaze gave me another reason for loving him for all time.

We fed the baby linnet until his crop bulged with Lea's fabulous Formula. In sharing his sleeping cage with the baby linnet, in playing for hours with the fledgling, Lorenzo remained gentle and friendly with the little bird until its release from the clinic two months later. Lorenzo actually seemed to know he was performing an important service. Through a sort of charismatic "I-dare-anybody-to-touch-that-linnet," Lorenzo helped us introduce the bird into our back-yard society. The jay sat for hours with the linnet until the little bird's peers accepted him (*him* because he had a bright-red chest, head, and shoulders) into their cho-rus of magnificent music makers.

Although the baby-linnet incident might be re-garded as an exception, Lorenzo's habits were for the most part *learned.* He acted out a bevy of memorized practices that might be called "reasoning." His leading me to the linnet was only one of many *reasoned* acts. People accustomed to his routines referred to his most intelligent performances as "development with human help." To which I counter with obvious fact: An animal's most memorized act requires some thinking in order to learn it in the first place. Almost instantly Lorenzo acquired the habit of stealing and hiding loot (insurance toward self-preservation later on), bathing, singing, and punishing offenses against him. But when we attribute any bird's behavior to "planning ahead," we get into deep water. Some habits are acquired more slowly: confidence in foster parents, clownish performances, and games. If Lea or I went to the kitchen— no matter where that glutton was in the house—he immediately dropped his busy work and followed. His mental associations were impeccable: kitchen plus people equaled food; Kaufman plus freedom equaled fun; big bully blue jay plus bully's mate equaled microwar; den plus loot equaled adventure. And so on.

We often accused Lorenzo of being in a rut. Through memorized routine, he ate the same foods in the same order almost every day, and if we failed to observe his system by changing that order, he fussed.

Month after month he uttered the same cries to express the same reactions to missing toys, shifted food routines, or physical changes in the house or garden. We recognize that all of these fixed acts were memorized and therefore habitually rooted—evolutionary in the eyes of good ornithologists. Instinct plus habit (salted with a little reasoning) equaled education. Olie the owl may have been a PE major, but Lorenzo was able to combine athletics and academics.

We still get a kick out of Lorenzo's simple mental gymnastics. Take hide-and-seek, with its complicated, planned deception. Try to assess that as pure instinct. How about luring birds into the cage doorway so he could peck their heads? The parakeet was neither first nor last to suffer Lorenzo's chicanery. How he would hide a cluster of objects, and later check his inventory and raise cain when one or more attractive articles had been substituted for the ones filched! He frequently came to our shoulders and "whispered," hoping to implicate either one of us or both in some dangerous dirty trick out-of-doors: annihilating a big jay-eating cat, routing raucous ravens that stole from his smorgasbord, drubbing his bully jaybird enemy, gunning down red-tailed hawks that dared any jay to come out in the open, putting up "security" for the loan of a neighbor's Phi Beta Kappa key that he had been unable to remove from its chain.

Our conclusion—based upon half a century of bird watching through the eyes of people-watching birds —was simpler than the findings of noted Audubonians: No sharp line separates instinct from reason. But there are subtle, observable differences.

Possibly as a means of sharpening either his instincts or his reasoning, Lorenzo found pleasurable challenge, indoors and out, in bringing toys to us to hide so that he could look for them. At least that was the way it seemed to Lea and me. He "hollered" if we made a searching task too difficult; he expressed impatience if we made it too easy for him. If that wasn't reason, I can't make another case for it. When Lorenzo suspected us of hiding something inside a clenched fist, he won the game fast because human flesh could not withstand that hammering beak for a full minute. If we went into another room to hide something from him—an article he had brought to us for hiding—he waited for us to call before starting his search. Strangely enough, he continued to retrieve the same article over and over again for rehiding. If we switched articles, he refused to search.

Sometimes we offered Lorenzo food he wanted intensely, such as buckwheat cake or bacon bits, when at the same moment he had a mouthful of something else. Hoping to prepare him for the time when he would assume year-round freedom in the jay-eat-jay world, we saw to it that he lost one of the two desirable choices if he trusted any living being with the other. We allowed him to hide what he had in his mouth but not to leave it in our charge and expect to find it when he had eaten the preferred tidbit. Other observers criticized this bit of training as badgering, but we believed that a little early badgering might save him many the empty gizzard later on.

Some writers have accused jays as a bird genus of robbing nests—eating other birds' eggs and tiny nestlings. Some even go so far as to say that jays are basically cruel, untrue to their mates, and act as sentries for other thieves in the wild. Without allowing our feelings toward Lorenzo to influence more than 98 percent of our thinking on that subject, we explored some of those claims. In more than half a century of observation, the odds are in the jay's favor that I should have seen at least one scrub jay robbing a nest. We have seen one documented photograph (in the, May 1984 issue of *Audubon*) of a jay taking a Baltimore oriole nestling from a nest. The jay depicted in the photograph was not a California species. For years California jays have reared their families on our property—in trees and shrubs within six feet of other species' roosts—and contrary to popular belief, we have yet to see a blue jay outrage another household. Disturb, yes; destroy, no.

During March—still famine time in birdland from

the standpoint of available food—each bird is hungry in his own wild corner. Should a renegade jay or any other aggressive species clean out a clutch of eggs at that time, don't fret about it; the young could not have survived in most American latitudes anyway, even if through some miracle the eggs did hatch.

From personal experience we can vouch that jays generally use reasonable care not to mangle the young of other birds when they prod nestlings in order to force them to regurgitate a recent feeding. Jays either gobble the upchuck themselves or take it to their own waiting offspring. Call it what you like, in jay circles of gutline survival it becomes "free enterprise." As a character, the jay may be rough and tumble, but he is too smooth an operator to wound the robin that coughs up the golden worm. In the eyes of his peers, the adult jay who robs chicks has violated none of *Nature's* laws. And so should we humans find a reason here for indictment? Survival values are to be applauded . . . though we may deplore nonhuman methods of achieving them.

As to constancy, the jay never steps out on a mate or leaves a consort while raising young. Mate-swapping may occur after a pair has produced a chick with defects; good genetics are at work. Some years jaycocks are in short supply—unpredictable as to when this will be. Scads of jayhens were attracted to handsome, well-fed Lorenzo, but not until his feathers matured, his clubfooted talons straightened out, and his twisted beak hardened true and shapely in his second summer. When the time came, however, our jay was to select a single mate and stay with her for more than nine years.

Within his developmental chronology, Lorenzo did what most normal jays did. He became everything that a jay was supposed to become; and being fowl, he had the right to cackle or crow as each situation developed in his favor as a result of his own efforts.

10

WE HAVE WATCHED JAYS, MAGPIES, and squirrels bury nuts and acorns in the damp soil both to hide the food and to soften the shells. They forget where they hide more than half the nuts until they see me pull out saplings after the spring rains. Jays bury stink beetles and dig them up two days afterwards because burial in damp ground eliminates the stink and ripens the tasty snack. I have never known a jay to forget where he buried a juicy stink beetle.

Tree-ripened fruit is delicious in the San Fernando Valley, but due to the law of supply and demand, birds and squirrels have to scrap for it. Therefore the jays, experts in meeting every environmental crisis (except smog), take to knocking plums, apricots, figs, pears, and peaches off the trees several days before the fruit is ripe. They conceal their harvests under grass and leaves, then recover it for a private feast when it has matured. Again, the exercise of free enterprise.

As I spade the flower beds twice a year and sift out bulbs and tubers, squirrel and jaybird treasure accumulates in the sifter. Likely to turn up are marbles, coins, silverware, pocket knives, keys, and other assorted hardware that was missed earlier. And if I have carelessly left my garage door open too many times, the consequences are even more evident.

Regular cleaning of Lorenzo's outdoor coop produced quantities of dead bugs, feathers of every hue, seeds, and assorted loot—mostly goodwill offerings that other birds had left in exchange for a share of the smorgasbord. This seemed to prove that he was not universally despised, although as a wheeler-dealer he may not have given value received. Outdoors he collected his own peculiar choices of plunder: mounds of shiny foil, bread crusts, nails, coins, glass gems, and mummified bugs. He always stacked his wealth neatly under the shredded paper with which we covered the floor of his cage. On hot days he used his water bowl for a bath tub, sometimes dumping the water after a bath and covering his hoard with the empty receptacle before coming indoors of an evening. For as long as he inhabited that coop, he remained convinced that backyard thieves regularly cleaned him out.

Hidden wealth under carpets and throw rugs in our house often shocked the wits out of guests who suddenly heard and felt crunches underfoot as they innocently stepped on Lorenzo's hidden booty. The eggshell–cracker–flashlight-bulb combination produced the best noise, and therefore the best facial expressions on guests. Lea and I unconsciously learned to walk around the little mounds because we knew what they contained.

Amazing surprises in hidden spoils piled up behind little-used volumes on bookshelves. Sometimes Lorenzo would stand and turn the pages of an unshelved book for fifteen minutes before dropping a nut meat, raisin, paperclip, snapshot, nail file, or a dehaired caterpillar. From the sugar bowl we sifted coins, buttons, safety pins, and one sugar-cured earthworm. A daily safari headed by two large red ants (we called them Stanley and Livingston) led a long file of bearers to food caches under furniture. Fall cleaning in our house came to be known as "harvest time"; we often recovered objects we didn't know we had. In such cases neighbors proved helpful in the identification and claiming of unfamiliar hardware.

After one such cleanup time, a well-meaning bird lover advised us to buy a larger cage to serve as Lorenzo's sleeping quarters on the service porch. The old cage was so small that the grown jay crumpled his tail feathers every time he perched and fell asleep. The local Woolworth's department store was advertising a bird-cage sale, so we took Lorenzo to the store to size him out for a new cage. Automobiles fascinated him; instead of trying to get out, he sat on my shoulder and "discussed" what he saw. When we arrived at the parking lot in North Hollywood, we put the jay in the old cage for transfer inside the store. Woolworth's was crowded with bargain hunters. Lorenzo did a slow "growl" when curious shoppers gawked and called him *cute*. Amidst the confusion, we assessed the large supply of sale-priced cages and came to a decision. But as we attempted to transfer Lorenzo from his old cage into the new one, the rogue made his escape. As our bird sailed back and forth from one end of the big department store to the other, everyone stared in disbelief. Children screamed and women flailed at Lorenzo with scarves and handbags. The louder the jay shrieked the more I panicked of course, but Lea stood calmly by, looking at her wristwatch, timing exactly how long it would take Lorenzo to find the jewelry department. Two minutes and thirty-seven seconds!

Jays do slow down a bit as they mature.

Customers registered mixed emotions when they discovered that Lorenzo was a tame bird. They saw him slip his beak into two rings and a bracelet, then return to my shoulder where he passed the jewelry to me for safekeeping. Howls of laughter went up when he repeated the performance as if it had been rehearsed. Lea said afterwards that my face was an iridescent beet-red. Several cynics expressed the opinion that the L.A.P.D. should know that I had coached the jay in shoplifting.

Lorenzo hated his new cage with a vengeance, so the store manager allowed us to return it, provided we did not come into the store again with "that hooligan bird." For many months the old cage remained his favorite nighttime roost and I suspect "security blanket."

In all discussions of jaybird loot, the question invariably arose: Did Lorenzo remember where he had hidden what? Indoors, yes. Outdoors, we are not sure. One of our reasons for wanting a larger cage was that we had rented a cabin in the mountains and wanted to take the jay along for a change of scenery and air. Because of sensitivity to the new environment—the smell of pine-scented, unpolluted atmosphere, the feel of altitude, the harkening to a medley of strange sounds such as thunderstorms, coyotes, and falling timber—our distressed bird never once left the cabin on his own. Although he was free to come and go with us, we sensed his tensions, stresses, and general heebie-jeebies.

After five days we returned home with our jay. He rushed at once to his parlor hoards, took all his mounds of toys and loot apart, and complained bitterly because we had thrown out several bits of reeking junk. On that same day he flew around the den a few times before settling on the desk lamp to eat bits from the small paper shade that we kept because of his early "sentimental" ties. At length he retreated to his own floorlamp shade where he tucked his head under his wing and went to sleep.

Like dime-store jewelry, many articles that Lorenzo brought to us for safekeeping were puzzling from the standpoint of what they meant to him. Oddly enough, he most often deposited each item either in a hand, or on a shoulder, or if small enough, inside an ear. He preferred that my hands hang onto his property until the time he decided to redeem it later for playtime acrobatics or simple hiding. Such behavior was similar no matter what the prize: apricot seeds, marbles, snail shells, gum wrappers, brass screws, plastic throwaways of all kinds, and shiny baubles. Accepting no substitutes for his deposits without a squabble, he demanded we hand back exactly what he had banked with us. With few exceptions he picked the correct (marked by me) item from any assortment set before him. From ten snail shells almost exactly alike he selected the marked one left in our care. Then, par for the course, he wanted the other nine.

Before making the rounds to count his mounting collection of stored wealth, Lorenzo habitually cast his beady glance over taboo areas (oven, desk drawers, camera bag, jewelry box), just in case someone had carelessly left one open and the coast was clear for a heist. He used Lea for a smoke screen for his behavior to come. Mussing up hair and tweaking earlobes diverted attention as he engaged in reconnaissance of portable trinkets and drafted a plan to snatch them. His dodges reached the stage of high art. He might draw tumultuous attention to a pretzel stick or after-dinner mint that he crammed behind a visitor's collar, but at the same time he kept a speculative eye on liftable doodads of potentially greater value. He surprised us dozens of times with his bizarre ability to distinguish between articles of value and plain junk. Blue jays are not supposed to possess the business acumen of a pawnbroker.

At maturity he was a veteran pirate with a preference for glistening, expensive loot that he associated with people. We figured he felt at home with human beings more than with other animals because the big two-leggers had rescued him from early misfortunes. He never forgot that *people* had saved him, loved him, amused him, and catered to his idiosyncratic wants. We know he enjoyed "soft-talking" into strangers' ears to let them know he was friendly and "relatively" harmless. When he was satisfied with food, property, and amusement (rare the day!), our bird extended friendly gestures to all nonpredators . . . he seemed to emphasize his own *minimum* of ulterior motives in that handsome head. He could have fooled a polygraph.

As an example of his collaboration with people, there were delightful times when Lorenzo postponed neighborhood looting and flew to one of us for simple companionship. Seeing Lea or me on a lawn chaise, the jay would drop from a utility pole or eucalyptus branch to a shoulder or an extended finger. We learned to recognize the times when he wanted to "talk something over" because the flow of jaybird chatter suddenly mounted to a crescendo. Someone said his voice was most "suffocating" when he looked to a human solution for one of his problems.

The plainest example of dialogue between Lorenzo and Kaufman was when both birds sang at the same time; the greatest "exchange of ideas" between Olie and Lorenzo seemed to occur when they yak-yakked in unison. Communication between man and bird was largely limited to the well-known "eye-talk" where "ideas" were exchanged through strong optical signals, best documented in the books of Lois Crisler. During eyeball to eyeball "chats" with Lorenzo, Lea and I did most of the listening.

When the talkative jay followed us about the house and garden, he flew alongside, gave out "happy-talk," or rode a shoulder while emitting a full steam of decibels (amounts of signal power equal to ten times the common logarithm of this ratio—I don't get it either, except that it hints of noise pollution). Others who have raised jays have told us of similar experiences. We fully believe that any genuine bird lover could duplicate the Lorenzo story by raising an orphan jay, using TLC and F.F.F.F.

Answer and rejoinder to our whistle and call were not exactly voluntary, nor was Lorenzo demonstrating obedience when he came to our beckon. Experienced bird people would label the behavior "conditioned reflex" because we so often reinforced the jay's responses with dog meat marinated in turkey gravy. We called it "conditioned deceptive arts." If he was busy unraveling Lea's knitting or dozing behind the water heater, he might fail to come, but he rarely refused to answer vocally. That meant he was not hungry at the moment. His answer to a persistent human call was the jaybird equivalent of "Go to hell!"

In any event it seems noteworthy that Lorenzo linked himself to human beings for companionship even when he was free to be with his own kind. He sailed into home port if he was within earshot of our call . . . provided he was able at the time to leave whatever project was engaging his attention. Notwithstanding the fact that he was people-raised, he remained at all times a nondomesticated animal. We deliberately discouraged any reaction that might lead to domestication such as remaining indoors or in the outdoor cage too long, although we never tried to suppress the cuddly or vocal affection he frequently demonstrated. His feisty attitude and cocksureness toward people manifested a genuine enjoyment of human company. Fortunately, I am happy to say that even the most anti-Lorenzo neighbors eventually accepted his colorful visits and friendly disposition—if not his vocal license. Free flight time increased, and he stayed away longer during part of the day, but he was back as usual when it came time for evening fun in the den.

People who have lived with an animal—wild or domesticated—recall the hours the pet would spend staring at his human host. Those who understand animals know that the creature did not stare unintelligently. He *studied* his complicated friend. What everyone recalls about a departed pet is the animal's responsiveness to human moods. The pet became that way through intensive study, most often while owners were unaware. And so it was with Lorenzo. As he listened to a human voice, he faced the speaker and paid amazing attention. It would be ridiculous to assume that jays understand human speech—they don't—yet Lorenzo displayed uncanny responses to our changing moods and activities as a result of the close study he made of human associates. He always recognized everyone he knew, but he may not have been aware of the vast differences among people, despite the depth of his study.

Of all the nondomesticated creatures we raised, none clung to dependence as Lorenzo did—yet none wanted independence as much as he did. The paradox resolved itself in knowing Lorenzo as an individual. Admittedly he had a good thing going under our roof. Even after maturity, he still identified with the baby jay, a state he was loathe to surrender: he squatted, crawled on his knobby elbows, and revolved like a break-dancer for jam on rye, peanut butter, ground meat, or chopped liver.

Even though we provided him with a plethora of goodies, however, Lorenzo proved beyond a doubt that he could take any kind of educational hard knock we might expose him to. When we began to withhold food on the smorgasbord trays, he found his own. The difference was perhaps the most dramatic discovery of his life: Local native food supplies were available only through competition. Could he or would he kill another of his kind for a meal? From the number of tugs-of-war on several lawns between Kaufman and Lorenzo, we believed the mocker must have extolled the dietary virtues of earthworms that Lorenzo only relished when very hungry. While sampling neighborhood fruit or turning over leaves for succulent bugs, the jay learned to keep his distance from a thoughtless child with a BB gun. The big bully Alpha taught our bird protocol by forcing him to use a distant birdbath instead of the one in our patio. Crows routed him when he tried to perch near Olie, the screech owl, and he discovered himself unwelcome in Fig Leaf Towers, where mated flock birds had taken a dislike to him earlier. A barn owl charged Lorenzo and knocked out a handful of feathers in a near miss on the Riverside Drive schoolhouse roof. Paired jays chased him from ripe apricot feasts; dogs barked through the fence at him; cars didn't stop for him on the street; worst of all, no living being paid him the kind of respect—not to mention attention—to which he was accustomed. He found it virtually impossible to assemble an applauding audience away from his own bailiwick. That was the bitter end! Even worse was the eye-opening discovery that it took a full day of hard work to find only a fraction of the food provided on his smorgasbord tray.

Helen Addison Howard, who had brought Lorenzo to us in the first place, said, "Instead of enrolling him in the School of Hard Knocks, you matriculated him in dear old TLC."

11

INTRASPECIFIC AGGRESSION IN A BIRD community indicates that an off-balance population is making adjustments. We freely use the cliché "as free as a bird," but any acceptable ornithologist will show you that every bird is a prisoner and runs a prisoner's risk of death the moment he flies beyond his or her assigned confines. That is what the newly introduced, hand-raised bird does *not* know. Even migrators that travel thousands of miles twice a year will return to their same flyways season after season and to their exact acreage, north and south, even though drought, fire, flood, or famine threaten to wipe them out.

Territorial circumstances, or "integrity," as it is sometimes called, are also linked irrevocably to a rigid hierarchy. Within given limits, Bird A somehow earns the right to peck all others among his or her ranks. Bird B can peck all but Bird A. Bird C, all but A and B. And so on down the social ladder to poor old Z whose fate it forever remains to sit and absorb right and left upper-pecks from the entire flock. Bird Z may not be a weakling or the village bonehead, but it appears that peckrights involve flock position of parents, personal ability to fight intelligently, pushiness, recklessness, even emotional charisma. Bird Z, although not necessarily the community hayseed, is not likely to operate with a high IQ. He keeps a low profile and simply avoids or absorbs the pecks of other flock members rather than fight.

Combat, even among doves of peace, takes place every time the members of one established community invade the air space of another group. Accordingly, under famine conditions on a forage range, survival may depend upon victory in internecine struggles or migration to the frontier of a species' natural ambit. These outer limits—zones of transition—provide fresh battlefields in which to establish new territorial integrity, sometimes with reshuffled peck rights. Underbird Z might even progress a notch or two. By refusing to migrate or move onto a new range, a few rugged individualists scrap it out on home territory.

So, we find a dead bird in the yard from time to time.

Unexplained belligerence within a species also rises and falls with seasonal challenges: mating, food specialties, amusement sources, shelter rights, security precautions, and—in the case of jays—intense love for dangerous adventure. One active force that prevents birds from annihilating the species from within is the meat-eaters—hawks, owls, eagles, falcons who take the old, infirm, and surplus young—nature's most efficient population balancers since life's watery dawn on this planet.

Lea and I never claimed to understand the fine points of territory, peck rights, or predation. We were simply raising orphans, realizing all along that we were fumbling with one of life's basic levers. I suppose if you look at it through the cold eyes of an evolutionist, a certain number of infant birds are presupposed to fall from their nests. Unless we freed a patient at the correct time, it established neither forage range nor peck rights and rarely survived even the first territorial skirmish. We learned the hard way. Little birds that we had grown to love fervently died horrible deaths before our eyes until we did the job according to Hoyle. For this reason we encouraged orphans to make initial flights and contacts with their own species as early as possible, provided most of those flights were taken during the brooding season, otherwise we held them over until the following year . . . or snuck them into the zoos.

Lorenzo was hatched in another community. Hence, from the beginning local jays regarded him as an escapee from a foreign bivouac, an impertinent squatter who horned in on another territory's wealth. So, when he ventured from his coop, they ganged up on him to settle peck rights, property rights, and mating rights, or to get rid of him entirely, which to the wild bird mind must have seemed most economical. Maybe that was the origin of the expression, "bird-brained."

When the going got too rough, Lorenzo simply scooted back to the food and shelter of his aviary. By encouraging his brief flights, by holding him over until his time for total freedom was just right, we exempted him, so to speak, from almost certain violent death until his neighborhood peers finally tolerated him. But it didn't mean that they liked him.

Lorenzo's flagrant talent for mischief may even have purchased his acceptability among fellow jays. We have seen him "dance" for joy inside his cage when he knew he had nettled another of his kind. In the eyes of his cousins, Lorenzo's most annoying habit was his feeding of itinerant linnets, sparrows, and starlings. He seemed to wait until his kin watched from the trees; then he would throw out fresh food to every passerine on the lawn in front of his coop. But let a jay knock on his door, and he would half-choke as he tried to gobble every smorgasbite, despite the fact that no other jay ever entered his huge enclosure to steal food from the trays.

Lorenzo was not partial to the flock birds. He incurred the enduring hostility of some by practicing ugly little offenses in order to aggravate them, sang off-key when linnets (masters of concert) and other real songsters sang in harmony, and broke out with inconsiderate whoops during afternoon siesta when all birddom respected quiet. On cloudless days, from the first light of dawn, you could hear birdland mutterings from all species as jays "flacked" up and down the community waking every living creature, including Lorenzo, still asleep on the service porch. Jays evolved to disturb the peace.

One afternoon in response to his emergency call, I ran out expecting to find at least a weasel on the loose. A diligent search revealed nothing. Planting himself near his door—locked because of a fight that morning between him and a larger jaycock—our jay pecked and gargled: his signal for me to let him out. Smelling a red herring, I opened the door.

He flew quietly (a new twist for Lorenzo) across the service yard and headed straight to the crows' nest on the top fork of Olie's sycamore. The pair of crows who occupied the nest had pecked the jay occasionally and with long beaks had reached through the wire mesh of his coop and gulped food from his trays. Through binoculars, I watched Lorenzo fly into the crows' nest and roll two eggs over the side with his beak! In a matter of seconds he was back on a perch inside his coop, once again as innocent as a da Vinci cherub. I *locked* the door of his cage.

Meanwhile, half a block away on Fulton Avenue the mated crows were cleaning up the remains of a red squirrel, a pedestrian casualty on that traffic-jammed thoroughfare. Within moments after returning to their nest, the enraged crows flew to our elm where the Alpha blue jay and his mate were dozing through a siesta. In no uncertain terms, the crows expressed their outrage. After chasing the jays all over the block, but without catching them, the crows finally withdrew to their empty nest and squawked until sundown. Then, as an afterthought before dusk, both crows flew down to inspect the door on a certain chicken-wire mesh coop.

Lorenzo crouched on a corner perch, feathers puffed out, head poked under a wing. Within a week the crowhen had laid another clutch of two eggs, but the pair never left the nest again at the same time until the young were hatched.

We still marvel that the crows narrowed their list

of possible suspects to the jaybird species within seconds after discovering the crime. It may have occurred to them that blue jays were also crow-related birds, the only species within forty miles—other than ravens—capable of shoving eggs over the rim of a nest. It may be that birds of one species recognize little or no differences among individuals of another generic family. One blue jay looks and sounds about as bad as the next to a crow—and the other way around. That apparently was the only identification available for the pair against whom Lorenzo committed the atrocity; those two crows carried out vengeful attacks against *all* blue jays for the rest of the summer.

Crows weren't the only bounders capable of sneaking up on jays. When red-tailed hawks soared down from the Santa Monica Mountains and described wide circles over the valley, magpies, mockingbirds, doves, blue jays, and pigeons—aware that their flights were slapdash compared to the hawk's—ducked for cover. Whenever a hawk drove the big bully Alpha into dense foliage, Lorenzo sat on his perch and "sang." Kaufman always hung around to add backup notes.

In his continuing love affair with mischief, Lorenzo also added voice to every kind of local warning . . . he even joined forces with other jays in noisy swoops against sparrow hawks (American kestrel) and cats, the closest approach we ever saw to cooperation with his jay-kind until he found a mate of his own. If one trait set Lorenzo apart at this stage—and frightened us—it was his ridiculous bravado in challenging furry animals. The dopiest cat on the block was a big old moth-eaten tom called Buzzy who lived next door and often stalked (but seldom caught) local birds. One morning the cat crouched to spring on Lorenzo. It was inevitable that the two should meet in confrontation. My neighbor chronicled the encounter:

"Lorenzo just stands there on the driveway. Feet wide apart, head low, feathers all puffed out like he's gonna take on the cat. When Buzzy leaps, Lorenzo takes off. At the same time he gives a peckin' to that dumb cat on the nose. Buzzy went over the fence like greased lightnin'."

Jays tease cats and dogs by flying in front of them to get their attention while other jays dive in and peck from behind, quite often for nest-lining material in the case of Persian cats. The results are sometimes fatal— to the jay. In addition to gambling with cats, Lorenzo picked up the habit of pecking dogs on the tongue when they tried to lick at his food through the wire mesh of his cage.

One afternoon Lea saw two German shepherds at the jay's aviary. Fortunately Lorenzo was under some kind of restraint at the time, so the door was locked. Lea said our bird pecked furiously through the mesh first at one canine nose then at the other, never giving an inch. Suddenly the two dogs charged the cage at the same time, causing it to crash from its foundation. A bowl of water, the smorgasbord trays, and several metal toys must have bounced off the jay's head. After chasing the dogs away, Lea found Lorenzo on his back, eyes closed, half-buried in shredded paper, puréed spinach, tapioca pudding, and chicken cacciatore. She rushed him to the service porch, washed him off, then brought him around with artificial respiration. She discovered that our jay was much easier to scrub while unconscious.

I arrived home about an hour after the episode. Woebegone Lorenzo sat perched on his lampshade where his story was about to undergo pompous magnification. A waking jay is never silent very long.

With intoned mutterings he flew to my knee and "told" me what had befallen him. That was the first evening when he undertook no creative demolition, and it was probably the only time in his adventurous career that he was truly submissive. After receiving my solemn sympathy he made a silent but dramatic exit to his sleeping cage where he spent the night without supper.

The following morning at five, his jubilant song filled the house as if nothing had happened.

The day after the German shepherd indignity, the jay

and I were jumping about on the front lawn like a pair of jackrabbits. That was the way we scared up the grasshopper harvest for the purpose of special food treats (run through the blender) for Kaufman and Lorenzo. Anyone who has tried blended grasshopper legs should explore a frontier of gourmet adventure with blended *whole* grasshoppers. It strained belief the way those two birds could eat basic blended grasshopper and hamburger meat, but neither bird was fast enough to catch grasshoppers without help. Kaufman sat on the roof's overhang and watched while Lorenzo and I did the jumping, flushing, swatting, and gathering. For a time it looked as if Lorenzo would eat up all the profits before we could blend the *pièce de résistance.*

All of a sudden Lorenzo rushed under a dense stand of honeysuckle to attack what looked like a big scaly snake. Our jay flew to the lawn, lisping wiry notes very different from his usual gravel-voiced "fight" rasp. While the ruckus on the front lawn brought neighbors to doors and windows to see what was going on, the reptile raced out in hot pursuit of the jay. It turned out to be a fourteen-inch-long alligator lizard, the kind we used to call "weekos." Weekos are fiercely aggressive lizards that live on insects, skinks, spiders, scorpions—even on small bird eggs. Lorenzo and his new enemy were all over the lawn, the jay in full battle retreat.

The fight recalled those terrifying old encyclopedia illustrations of Mesozoic struggles between dinosaurs. The weeko stood on his hind legs and leaned against his tail like a miniature *Tyrannosaurus rex*. His jaw snapped closed with a vicious pop every time he charged the nervy jay. Lorenzo fought by flapping into the air like a gamecock, by pecking and footing up and down the lizard's back, by trilling his shrillest war cry. At length from the safety of a rosebush, he broadcasted for reinforcements. Before I could run for a stick to lift the weeko out of range, the big Alpha blue jay, his mate, and Kaufman descended upon the lizard.

The weeko, outflanked and outsmarted, wisely retreated into the honeysuckle. Lorenzo abandoned the grasshopper harvest, flew to his coop, and "growled" for the rest of the day. Kaufman and the other two jays spent hours hopping and flopping around the honeysuckle vine where they rehashed the encounter, continuously challenging and intimidating the weeko to a return match. The Alpha jay may have cooperated with Lorenzo because of the last red-tailed hawk warning that our jay had sounded. Occasional cooperation didn't mean yielding any of his *número uno* status.

Everyone—from hummingbirds to humans—recognized that Lorenzo always scrambled for the coop the moment he detected a "misfire" in his natural environment. If he sounded the alarm with repeated "flacks," we rushed out as a matter of reflex. Other jays would converge upon the yard at his call, which meant he had achieved certain status himself. It never seemed to matter to his allies how many times—out of boredom, we suspected—he yelled "Wolf!" when no wolf impended. Sometimes we thought he blew the whistle simply to test the alertness of his confreres. After being locked up for an accumulation of reasons until he cooled off, he would bring a toy to the cage door as if offering bail for the freedom he must have known he could not yet handle on a full-time basis.

Lorenzo may have *caused* ulcers, but he never *got* any.

The day after the weeko free-for-all he played upon our sympathy, making it clear that he had big-time reasons for wishing to stay indoors all day. This was very much against our program for his permanent release. He "wailed" every time I started for a door with him on my shoulder. He clung to my hair with beak and talons, "hummed" as he rode to the clothesline in the service yard. Once yielding to his secret reasons for remaining indoors, Lea and I spent the rest of the morning cleaning up the messes he made. Accordingly, by noon we were both so worn out trying to keep up with his destructive behavior and untidy habits that we feared he might have received brain damage from overstimulation in one of his recent brawls; therefore, we paid the veterinarian to X-ray the bird's head for possible fracture or concussion.

Once more we gave the vet an opportunity to wink at his assistant when he handed us his statement for Lorenzo's loss of face during the weeko battle.

12

WE HAD BARELY RECOVERED FROM THE financial setback imposed by the veterinarian when we decided to have a few friends over for dinner. For obvious reasons we generally locked Lorenzo in his cage when we invited dinner guests. That evening, however, at visitor insistence, we covered the den furniture with clean linen and limited the jay's activities to that room. There were no accidents. Just song, coin mooching, purse burglary, wig-lifting, jewelry thefts, and—for noncontributors to his tidy bundle of assets—pecks to the napes of their necks.

If you are ever short of a party conversation piece, introduce a blue jay!

During dinner the neglected bird sustained an un-varying "Flack! Flack! Flack!" Finding himself iso-lated in the den and knowing that the action had shifted to the dining room, naturally he tried to join the company. Lea thought *I* had slammed the door between the den and the kitchen, I thought *she* had taken that chore upon herself. The jay had learned earlier that unless a door was snapped closed, he could fly against it several times and open a crack through which he could squeeze into the next room. I heard his body thumping repeatedly against the door.

As Lea made her way towards the dining room, carrying a triple-layer coconut-marshmallow cake, Lorenzo opened his door between the kitchen and the den. To my wife's surprise, that bird flew to her shoulder and bugled a triumphant entry into the din-ing room, where he could rejoin the laughing guests. There wasn't much Lea could do about it because she needed both hands to hold the dessert. But her expres-sion was grim.

When she placed the glowing masterpiece on the Lazy Susan centerpiece, Lorenzo dived from her shoulder to the top of the cake. An inch of coconut and marshmallow icing made a gooey landing site even for agile Lorenzo. In order to keep his balance he waded around on the cake, halfway up to his knees, dragging his midsection, spreading his marshmallowed wings and tail. Then bogged down hopelessly, like a fly in molasses, he demonstrated an original meaning of the term *savoir-faire:* the blighter began to sing and eat at the same time!

Bird and cake were declared a disaster area.

With disciplined Swiss calm, Lea hustled the writhing mess back to the kitchen. The guests were holding their sides. Squawks, running water, and vocabulary

(the short, explosive variety not often heard in the "Loonybin") made it clear that Lorenzo was undergoing a none-too-gentle scrubbing under the faucet. In a matter of five minutes, Lea, all smiles, and the cake —minus Lorenzo, minus most icing—reappeared on a wave of dry giggles.

If we tempted our jay with such an attractive arena for adventure as a coconut-marshmallow cake, we'd foot the bill for the consequences—with reservations. We accept our feathered associates as they are, not as we would always like them to be. As a friend, Lorenzo wore well throughout the time we knew him. Even after repeated social errors, we were determined to protect his vanity and verve. If we had to wear towels around our necks because he was not housebroken, we wore towels. We were not about to submit him to training that was unnatural for a bird. I don't honestly believe his life with us altered his native personality one bit.

But he certainly altered ours!

According to Mohammedan legend, several mischievous animals have gone to heaven: Jonah's big-mouthed whale, Noah's wayward dove, and at least two frisky jackasses. Each of those creatures was engaged in a delight-making combo with human partners.

We'd like to nominate Lorenzo—at least for consideration.

During a bird's training period for release, we never conditioned it to meanness by teasing. We believe that deliberate pestering or teasing during any kind of training reflects bankrupt imagination on the teaser's part and results in no value to the animal. One of Lorenzo's own countless pleasures, nonetheless, was to tease—better said, perhaps, to play practical jokes. To our knowledge, no animal other than fellow jays ever deliberately tormented Lorenzo as the butt of a joke, such as chasing, out-yelling, and stealing his toys. But Lorenzo repeatedly dropped things (on purpose) on the human head and looked back for the effect as he flew away—a form of joke or tease. For pure cussedness he shuffled a deck of cards into four rooms, pecked holes in toothpaste tubes, and tore typewritten manuscript pages. But we weren't about to punish him, even if we had thought it would have done any good. Lea and I were permissive, given that sanity was no prerequisite to our trade.

Either as a tease or a joke, Lorenzo got special kicks at night from silently plundering an unlighted room where he often stole more than he could carry. He had the cheek to bring his loot to the den where he scattered it unless he was in a mood to hide it. Sometimes he hovered over a bar of perfumed soap that he couldn't lift but refused to give up on. A garbled distress signal from the pantry meant that pilfered peanut butter had the joke on him; when this happened, we were obliged to rush to his aid with eye-droppersful of milk. One night, after scrambling to his cry from a bathroom, I found the jolly gent entangled in a mound of toilet tissue he had unrolled in the dark. I can still see that rakish head poking out from yards of paper.

He no sooner got untangled than he swooped into Lea's bedroom and landed on her dressing table. We suspected devilment when he returned several times to the den, his breath reeking of Shalimar. Every few minutes he hopped or flew back when he thought we were looking only at our reading matter. Flying in-doors was too high visibility, so if he was engaged in a real heist, he hopped to the scene of his delinquency. We snooped when things began to fall. There in the moonlight tiptoed Lorenzo, skidding about on every third step across the marble-top vanity, standing so high he looked like a miniature stork. His neck was stretched like the arm of a farsighted person examining fine print. He had overturned cosmetics and sampled everything that spilled; best of all, he favored Shali-mar. Once aware of our snooping, he made off to the living room with a fingernail file that required two months to find.

Short-fused and dead set on changing the subject after being apprehended, he flew to my shoulder and chiseled the back of my neck. He "back-talked" with

impudence when we shamed him but soon forgot the issue. He never retired angry to his sleeping perch. Disturbed at times with markedly hurt feelings, but never angry. But for days, Lea was angry every time she walked past that cage and still smelled Shalimar.

And speaking of Lorenzo's service porch cage without a door, for ease of moving around we hung it next to a shelf where Lea kept her cleaning supplies. Our bird, by nature given to oddball tastes, relished a few hefty bites of Fels Naptha soap. The texture may have reminded him of chewing gum. After an early morning slurp from a vessel of liquid detergent and a bite of Fels Naptha, he blew opalescent bubbles every time he drank for the rest of the day. Later he tried milk and produced, among other things, frighteningly opaque foam. He became irritated when we laughed at a triple bubble, one from his mouth and two from his nostrils at the same time. And then the jay was quick to turn his mistake into burlesque. He blew rainbow-tinted bubbles, then reached up with a foot to pop them. This was one of several times we observed in Lorenzo a cackling reaction that may have been similar to human laughter.

In the record book of the jay's daily exploits, we recorded curious anecdotes told by young people whom we engaged on rare occasions as birdsitters. We told each sitter that Lorenzo would have to learn fear before we could release him permanently, so one sitter took it upon herself during our absence to educate him in that area. She tried fast movements in his direction with strange objects from her handbag. Unaware of his keen-witted ability to get even, she made the mistake of presenting the same "scare" twice. On the second time around, neither the object nor the movement was strange, so the jay pecked her hand when she failed to come up with a new scare. He probably thought the game was great. During one scuffle through the den, the walls, carpeting, and Lorenzo received weird-orange streaks from a lipstick he had quick-tricked from her handbag.

Beyond reach on the dining room chandelier, he tore up a love note the girl had folded into a sailplane and thrown at him. She declared him unteachable when her tiny compact slipped from the jay's beak and smashed on the tile floor in a bathroom.

As he approached adulthood, Lorenzo ate between one-quarter and one-third of his weight each day, often more . . . he had a lordly way of backing off, raising his head high, and turning when his crop began to bulge. That meant "No more, thank you." Regardless of how full he was, though, if he saw someone bite into food with which he was unfamiliar, he demanded a sample. If refused what he considered his fair share, the jay waited until the refuser started to chew with his or her mouth open, as adolescent birdsitters are wont to do.

Food was perhaps the only business that ever caused Lorenzo to become 100 percent serious.

Absorbed by the prospects of another evening away from home, we neglected to caution a birdsitting boy about Lorenzo and food. The boy, to whom we had given refrigerator privileges, said later that the bird could strip a chicken drumstick almost as well as he could. Lorenzo dropped what he was eating as soon as the boy began chewing on something new. Bird and boy proceeded to wash down every other bite with Coca-Cola from the boy's glass.

Upon returning home, we found both boy and bird sound asleep on the sofa in the den.

Because of student interest in academic nature mov-
ies and in often-told tales by our birdsitters, one neighborhood schoolteacher invited us to visit her class-
room and bring Lorenzo to demonstrate what we had
done with native wildlife. In light of what we contributed to general pandemonium at the school that
afternoon, we concluded that Lorenzo's visit should
not have coincided with such attractive scholastic activities as finger painting, peanut rolling, and under-
water basket weaving. Lorenzo never had such a ball.
I'll take an oath that nobody learned anything!

We dared believe that the bird may have picked up
several bad habits from the schoolchildren. We deplored the way he began strafing the heads of our
guests and singing with a mouthful of hominy grits
after the schoolroom fiasco. But in a sense we finally
agreed that a bright-blue spirit was far more important
than social graces. As a young bird, he gobbled what
he could swallow until he was full, rarely showing
even temporary likes and dislikes. Even as an adult he
sometimes ate everything but food: playing cards,
snapshots, paper napkins, book matches, lard, soap. He
considered it a special treat to lick the ink from a
ballpoint pen. As he began to enjoy the taste of his
meals, he choked less on man-sized bites he had been
in the habit of seizing from our forks and plates. At
long last he learned to eat for pleasure rather than for
quantity competition. As a mature bird—an individ-

ual of extraordinary speed and stride at our competitive table—he could grab peas, sauerkraut, or syrup-dunked pancake from any fork that journeyed at a good-taste rate of motion between plate and human mouth.

We had to give up summer breakfast and other meals on the outside patio, not on account of Lorenzo's abominable table manners, but because he "invited" his jaybird pals. A blue jay in the garden accepting a peanut from your hand is one thing; a brazen foursome stormtrooping your table—plate, cup, glass, fork, and *mouth*—is an abuse to be endured only by the hair-shirt set.

It was never a question of approval when Lorenzo tromped around inside a sugar bowl or took shortcuts through a plate of tamale pie. We simply refused to frustrate or restrain a heritage destined for early independence in the rough-and-tumble outside world.

A neighbor was forced to feed his dog indoors because a "flock" of jays regularly descended at meal-time and aced the poor mutt out of her groceries. Through our generally reliable neighborhood grape-vine, we heard that Lorenzo was also involved in the dogfood conspiracy.

Joybird that Lorenzo may have been in our house—at our table, bed, and bath—he never knew complete freedom from personal conflicts. One of his unreasonable fears involved the mail carrier's uniform, whistle, and jeep, which never failed to bring out Lorenzo's prejudices, quirks, and petty notions. His reaction was always consistent: loud and intolerant yaks with eloquent pauses between. We finally came to the conclusion that Lorenzo's "fear" was another masterpiece of attention-getting. When we are studying an animal's behavior, it is sometimes difficult to tell the difference between what is meaningful to the animal and what is insignificant . . . too many times human feelings intrude despite our best intentions to be objective.

Why, for instance, should a new red shirt with black squares become a dangerous monster to Lorenzo? And subsequently to every jay in the neighborhood? Indoors our bird refused to stay in the same room with the shirt even when I stuffed it under a sofa cushion. Later I wore it to the Santa Monica Mountains where there lived a colony of California jays. It was a chilly day and the birds were hungry; however, not one dared to approach for chopped walnuts until I removed and hid the shirt. This behavior, while universal among jays, appeared more attributable to dislike than fear.

We thought that Lorenzo's abnormal foot accounted for oddball behavior now and then: stumbles and several hang-ups. He often reeled as if unable to get purchase on flat surfaces, like a sailor with shaky sea legs trying to negotiate a slick dance floor, at which time the jay slowly turned his head and walled his eyes to see if Lea or I intended to help him get his balance. If we even noticed the handicap, he sassed, pecked, and pouted. If we laughed in spite of ourselves at his clumsy fall or the off-key wheeze that went with it, he appeared to pretend that the performance was deliberately comic. He repeated the gauche auditions that we learned to accept as probable attempts to get a "laugh in the fast lane." He pretended inability to get up after a "fall," exaggerated staggering with wing flutters and phony limping that soon deteriorated into the "broken" wing act. All this faking eventually ended in vocal displays: the blue jay's court of final appeal. Like every jay I have ever observed, Lorenzo remained a ham to the core.

On the other hand, he had a small private collection of situations where giggling was unthinkable.

After the coconut-marshmallow cake botch-up, we thought Lorenzo was immune to insult until we laughed one evening at his growing repertoire of "mood music." He simply embarked without preliminary conditioners upon the long, sad notes of "blue soul." Our thoughtless guffaws caused him to leave the den and retire early to his sleeping cage—not angry, but apparently wounded . . . for a short time.

He muttered if anyone snickered when he emerged from a bath, perhaps because he habitually conversed seriously with himself as he strutted away from his

tub. Wet, sloppy, and unjaylike, he was barely less conspicuous than a jaybird on a layer cake. We cautioned visitors not to laugh or make humorous remarks until Lorenzo had squeegeed his feathers or until Lea had curried him down with an ersatz sponge.

Many times he performed inexplicable specialties peculiar to Lorenzo alone: deliberate sitcom, companionship with Kaufman and Olie, risqué liberties taken with "married" jayhens, one-way "conversations." When he did something original that he liked—or that drew any degree of applause—he quickly added the act to his stockpile of performances, whether anybody else liked it or not.

With woodpecker talent for doing certain things the hard way, Lorenzo also developed several quirks. We kept his regular toys in a well-anchored matchbox that he could easily open, yet somehow he acquired the notion that the sides had to be pecked before he could pull slightly on the inner compartment in order to inventory his property. He refused to open the box without first giving it a hammerhead or two.

Another example of the woodpecker way: When his neck or head itched, he stood on one foot, reached around behind a wing, opened his beak, and performed an Olympian scratch. The scratching leg worked between wing and body! Other birds simply kick forward to abrade an itch.

I watched him work endlessly trying to insert a candy Lifesaver into a pipe bowl where it couldn't possibly fit. When he failed to shove a spool of thread into a conch shell, he moped and "whined" because I wouldn't help him. Then he pouted and grouched because a bottle cap refused to go through the mouth of the bottle he saw it come from.

Try as we might, we never understood the full significance of specific obsessions. Occasionally Lorenzo stood under the little desk lamp whose shade he often nibbled. If the light was on, he stared at the bulb until he was hypnotized, after which he fell over stiff. When this happened, he required roughing up and head cooling with an ice cube in order to bring him out of his trance.

13

WHEN WE AGREED TO RAISE LORENZO we knew little about the roughneck personality and happy-go-lucky lifestyle of the species. We knew jays only as noisy backyard visitors—scrappy, bold, and fearless. Like pet pythons, Limburger cheese, and parachute jumping, blue jays are an acquired taste. Nevertheless, we have met an increasing number of jaybird fanciers, if not fans. Several people who have raised them as household or garden pets came to ring our doorbell. No one noted any conspicuous differences between their jays and ours . . . same behavior during chickhood, same agile brains during development, slightly different anecdotes.

One such fan, Walter Harris, accompanied by a Steller's (crested) jay he had raised from an eggling, toured the United States in a recreational vehicle. The jay took in the scenery from a special perch at windshield level above the passenger seat in an air-conditioned cab, and caused considerable gawking in traffic. According to Harris, the jay thoroughly enjoyed the trip. When I saw this jay's magnificent crest of topknot feathers, I felt momentarily sorry for Lorenzo who—at that time prior to first moult—still had little besides scar tissue on top of his head. A California jay has no crest, but can hackle his body plumage in anger, petition, fright, surprise, sleep, or during a snatch— just as a dog hackles the hair along its spine. Harris said his Steller's jay was equally at home in the mountains, at the seashore, on the desert, or in the city. In the wild, Steller's jays rarely leave mountain pine forests.

Another acquaintance, Albert Zanini, raised a brood of six California jays that he had removed from a nest when the mother was shot by a youngster with a pellet gun. After raising Lorenzo, I could only vaguely imagine what *six* blue jays could accomplish under one roof, if indeed the roof remained for very long. Fortunately, there was no Mrs. Zanini. Our friend stated with a straight face, "I've turned the house over to the jays and they have refused to leave, although they are well past maturity. As a matter of record, several have brought in mates!"

"We understand," Lea said. "We turned our house over to *one*." How could Lea possibly understand?

Zanini claimed that jealousy was a devastating factor in a multiple-jay home. He assured us—and we accepted his statement without further corroboration —that six jays could think up more mischief than six-times-one alone. The man looked and acted as if he needed a tranquilizer.

Not long after Zanini's visit, an elderly woman from Pasadena herded her 1930 Packard roadster all the way to the San Fernando Valley (twenty-four miles) to meet Lorenzo. She sobbed and wept as our boisterous jay put on one of his best shows. It was a new experience for Lorenzo to see someone cry. At length he waddled up and hopped to the woman's outstretched hand. As she held him near her face, he leaned over and sipped a tear that was about to drop from her chin. Apparently Lorenzo didn't savor tears, because he spat it right back onto her face, after which he cocked his head from side to side and buzzed like a bumblebee. Luckily the woman took his performance in stride. The jay listened without interruption while she told her story.

"Our bird, Mr. Ramshaw, was a jay just like you,"

she said to Lorenzo. "He brought sunshine into our home from the day we picked him up as a fallen nestling. He had complete freedom of the house and all out-of-doors. Mr. Ramshaw was singing at the top of his lungs when he dropped dead. Sixteen years old!"

We have heard of several jays that outlived their time of ten to fifteen years: all of them were hand-raised.

Thus, Harris, Zanini, and the woman from Pasadena —examples of the many "blue jay people" who rang our doorbell during Lorenzo's tenure—told virtually the same story of a species that should have been called *joybird*.

While each jay was a strong individualist, each had characteristics that were the same or similar. For instance, when Lorenzo landed on any part of the human body, he made polite little Japanese bows. It seemed that all "household" jays did the same thing. If our jay sensed uneasiness when he alighted on a visitor's shoulder, he sneaked around behind and grabbed an earlobe to intensify the person's discomfort before making friends. Other jays did the same. Children were flabbergasted at the way Lorenzo walked around on their shoulders, arched his neck, and hummed high-pitched notes through his nostrils. Teenagers who saw him bow before and after speedy bowel movements were always nervous when he lit on their shoulders or hands, where he went through bowing gestures whether his bowels moved or not.

Young visitors often confronted us with the question, "Why does he stick around and put up with that chicken coop when he could fly away?"

We believe he stuck around because he liked what he had: food, shelter, amusement, protection, attention, feathered friends, love, and—perhaps most of all —an appreciative audience. If during his maturing months he ever had a notion of leaving, all he had to do most of the time was flap his wings and go. But he didn't. Lorenzo's instincts, not the cage, kept him as our ward until his internal clock informed him that the hour of his natural fulfillment had arrived.

14

I'LL ADMIT WE HAVEN'T ALWAYS KEPT
our birds until the clock struck the exact hour for
release. After seeing several killed by their own species,
however, we recognized the importance of proper
introduction to the wild habitat. For a time we kept
them too long. There had to be a correct answer. More
times than we admit, we transported a linnet, white
crown, vireo, towhee, or thrush beyond the turnstiles
of the Los Angeles and San Diego Zoos. The abun-
dance of uneaten food lying about, protected grounds,
good climate, only half-stratified bird societies, and

people in a relatively respectful frame of mind toward animals seemed to us a better environment for newly released birds than the interurban battleground of our backyard. As far as smaller birds were concerned, the idea was not a bad one. But there must be a better answer.

One frightening thing, for which our custody was in large measure responsible and about which we could do so little, was the development of trust in human beings. Lorenzo or any other inpatient or out-patient would surely be a tempting target for a boy with a BB gun as the bird perched on a fence post and sang its trillingest song.

But we had to face the fact that complete freedom was the birthright of all these birds: their legacy from the hour they could handle liberty's problems and responsibilities. As Lorenzo's hour approached, the oldest law of nature made itself known: Liberty minus responsibility equals extermination—but quickly. We fretted because we knew that while Lorenzo lived with us, he was a displaced bird. Without regard for personal feelings, our policy has been to give full freedom to wildlings as soon as they are educated to make it on their own. That was the goal behind our tutelage, the one and only reason for operating the clinic.

So, as Lorenzo's hour drew near we saw to it that

he sat more in the elm and acacia, less in his cage. By habit more than by choice, I suppose, he returned freely to the coop if an enemy chased him. He continued to fly to our door for his evening of indoor fun and his sleeping cage. His shrieking tantrums now were triggered when we excluded him both from the house and the outdoor coop. He wasn't about to get used to the idea until his internal computer printed out the message.

With a starry-eyed notion that we were weaning the three of us, we tried farming him out with people who volunteered to host him for a week or two. We sent him away each time in his sleeping cage. Without exception the cage reappeared the next day with a single comment: "Here's that awful bird." Confused Lorenzo had looted every home into which he was introduced. Instead of going to a favorite lampshade, he perched wherever he pleased and marked the spot with copious droppings. Not about to roost for the night in his sleeping cage, he filled each host's residence with strident shrieks that went on nonstop into the wee hours.

Because new fledgling inpatients were entering the clinic late that second spring of Lorenzo's life, we finally took the jay to a veteran blue jay lover who lived about a mile from us at the foot of the scrub-oak-covered hills. Our friend, Agnes Day, was known throughout the Valley as a woman of true Franciscan charity when it came to birds. She agreed to keep him until he was ready for permanent release. Lorenzo, always delighted with a ride in the station wagon, didn't realize he was leaving for good. After a tearful goodbye we slowly returned home to our latest charges, already missing that bright confederate. When I drove onto the driveway, Kaufman was prancing up and down the carport's shingled ridgerow singing everybody else's song but his own. Several jays, unnaturally silent, flitted about the garden as if looking for something. Barnaby and his mate were helping themselves to my half-ripe apricots, and Fig Leaf Towers literally shook with nestlings begging their parents for lunch.

There on the patio table, shaking an impish head, stood Lorenzo! The bounder had gotten home before we did because he flew as his cousins the crows fly. We were so glad to see him that Lea gave him one of her prize pickled figs, which he took to the rooftop and shared with Kaufman.

With the exception of raptors, hand-raised jays released at maturity can care for themselves better than most species. The blue jay's eat-everything-insight habit and his invasive behavior lead to a high survival rate among releasees. Superb intelligence coupled with determination to occupy his own niche make for quick adjustment to weather, natural enemies, and competition for available food. Longer periods outside the coop, fewer kitchen-prepared smorgasbites, less handling, and fewer drop-everything responses to vocal demands finally brought about Lorenzo's weaning. As a general rule, home-raised jays should receive complete freedom in late spring or early summer when wild pairs are concerned more with brooding than newly introduced competitors. This varies by neighborhood, with greatest hostility toward newcomers in areas of densest blue jay population. Any bird will face its most serious problems with its own species.

No matter how peaceful a backyard may appear to human eye, to any wildling the site bristles as a battle-ground . . . a living web, balanced down to the last ladybug. A new bird's entry into that "free" society sends silent signals followed by noisy war cries throughout the surroundings. Woe to any conspicu-ous newcomer! Birds tolerate overpopulation of other species but will defend a territory, even to death, against one new kindred member moving in to com-pete for living space and food supply. Young adults are supposed to disperse from their birthplaces and find unoccupied territorial niches. Next to peck rights, food and housing problems remain top priorities. In-terspecific strife, while a factor, is rarely an important issue in the introduction of a Lorenzo-type bird with proper exposure prior to release: limited free-flight time increased, a few intraspecific fights permitted, lengthy outdoor housing in a high-visibility cage. If wild birds are accustomed to seeing and hearing an "alien," they are most apt to accept him upon release.

With all his handicaps behind him—beak, clubbed foot, and bald head—Lorenzo was ready to hack it on his own. When he wised up to his natural vocation of earning his own living, nature demanded that he give up his foster home. So, he put in fewer calls at the

smorgasbord tray, which he must have noticed contained less and less food . . . until at last all magic in
the cornucopia ceased to exist. His native diet—fresh
fruit, seeds, insects, worms, slugs, tiny vertebrates,
acorns, and nuts—suddenly acquired natural appeal. In
order to find that sustenance, he demanded that he be
out-of-doors from dawn to sunset.

As Lorenzo's second autumn arrived, we noticed a
neat little yearling jayhen, a newcomer in our block,
who disregarded protocol and either sat on the
wooden platform (landing strip) in front of Lorenzo's
coop or went inside and perched next to him. For two
weeks she panicked and fled to the acacia when Lea or
I came near the cage. Each day she became tamer until
at length she came for peanuts when we called
"Loretta!" She ate from my hand because she had seen
Lorenzo do so with impunity. The two birds jabbered
as if a lifetime would not be long enough in which

to say it all. They chattered in muted lisps and creaky gurgles from sunrise to sunset.

"Here's *that bird* again!" Lea said each day with just a trace of scorn when she saw the two of them together in the coop, in the garden, or in the neighbor's fruit trees. Lea and I simply turned our eyes from the handwriting on the wall. When Lorenzo didn't protest after Loretta grabbed and hid his peanuts, we knew our little hero was hooked.

Since winter, rapidly approaching, was possibly his most dangerous foe, we had hoped to keep Lorenzo indoors on rainy and frosty nights. We hated to deprive him of warm evenings in the den where he had known such fun, but orphan fledglings of other species now occupied all available space in the clinic and most of our attention. When the day came, however, for us to remove Lorenzo's coop from the backyard, we removed it without hesitation and with no regrets. We recognized—as Lorenzo must have—that the time was right. So, his day of truth was 21 November, not as one day but as a culmination of days. Autumn moult had resulted in a gorgeous head of real feathers where only scars and baldness had been before. His fluffy Loretta fanned the spark that demanded a move, and we hoped they would increase their noble, if often roguish, tribe. Loretta led her mate to the nearby Santa Monica Mountains where she introduced him to his ancestral feast of scrub oak acorns abundantly ripe in November. All local jays had gone to the acorn harvest.

Naturally we missed his rousing greetings, nonstop voice, and atrocious manners. I missed the rascal's confidence in me as custodian of his booty. We missed his raucous afternoon call when he became lonely. And I can tell you right here, during his first week away, we reacted much like that woman from Pasadena.

But his story has a natural ending . . . better said, a natural beginning. We suspected that Lorenzo would not stay away very long because, as we surmised, on the wilderness stage with its meager audiences, that jay could never find the amount of applause he needed.

Sure enough, at the end of three weeks here came the noisy pair, having abandoned natural haunts in the brushy chaparral-covered hills. As Loretta hopped about the patio, fizzing with a sound exactly like an agitated Coke, Lorenzo hammerheaded the back door for one of us to open it. While he visited and "told" us his adventure yarns, his mate fumed and fussed in the elm. From the den we could hear her husky-voiced clamor.

The pair roosted now in our backyard trees, but there was never another evening visit from Lorenzo. I suspected as much when I saw him eyeing all the new inpatients.

During the first chilly rains of December, we paced the floor worrying about those two birds. Where did they go? How did they stay dry and warm?

Being better prepared for their freedom than we were, Lorenzo and Loretta did the rational thing, of course. They perched on a dry shelf under the roof's overhang next to the warm bricks of the chimney. At 6:00 A.M., he and his mate shrieked for hot oatmeal, complete with sugar and cream, which—need I add? —they received in copious amounts. Both birds, now inseparable, shivered in the morning chill, but both declined an invitation to come indoors. The wild had adjusted its own.

In our backyard the pair put up with fewer indignities from the big bully Alpha jay. The latter soon experienced several telling jabs from Lorenzo's fully mature, protruding mandibles, backed by Loretta's fearless power dives.

Now that Lorenzo had a mate, we thought he would certainly terminate his unusual friendship with the mockingbird Kaufman. If anything, the bond between the two unrelated species became stronger than ever, especially after Kaufman himself overwhelmed a mate.

Lorenzo's mating caused no flurry among other backyard wildlings. Twice we saw our jay take Loretta to Olie's door, but the owl refused to come out. Olie was never very friendly with Lorenzo after our bird had destroyed the crows' eggs . . . and, too, Olie had proved himself scornful of all association with females, regardless of species. Loretta snubbed Barnaby by ignoring his existence. She power-dived the squirrel a few times when he dug up jay-hidden peanuts and walnuts; otherwise, she somehow influenced Lorenzo also to have no truck with squirrels. Other nonmigrators seemed satisfied to look the other way when the jays asserted themselves.

On Christmas morning Lorenzo and Loretta sat on a utility pole across the street. They were shaking the Christmas Eve mist from their feathers before coming to my hand for chopped nuts and raisins. Suddenly I saw two teenage boys sneak beneath the wires. They eyed the jays, looked up and down the street, then withdrew slingshots from their jackets, loaded them with marbles, and were about to draw bead on the birds. I raced across the street. Slingshots were strictly forbidden within the city limits. I solemnly promised not to call the police if the boys would relinquish their weapons in exchange for two small bird feeders and a supply of grain that Lea and I kept for such occasions. My wife put a bit more "spirit of Lorenzo" into the educational message she delivered when the boys' parents telephoned in a futile attempt to recover the slingshots—by then in live embers where Lorenzo had hidden the woman's wig.

When Lorenzo left our hearth we felt the void, but

when he and Loretta decided not to nest in the hills —to return to our property with all their fearless, metallic sass—we felt that our friendly association had produced worthwhile results. As the two jays sailed from tree to tree, they looked as if they had been invented by the Creator in a lighter moment. Logically we might have expected the pair to move elsewhere at nesting time, but Lorenzo apparently still considered elm and acacia his territory. We did feel a twinge, however, that neither bird ever revealed to us their exact nesting site, where Lea was fully prepared to deliver F.F.F.F. The elm and acacia were very old and tall trees, densely foliated. Although both jays always flew into the elm, movements and inevitable sounds told us that the nest was in the acacia. We knew enough not to violate one of Lorenzo's untouchable secrets. Many a dish of F.F.F.F. was cleaned of its contents, but the destination of the food was Lorenzo's and Loretta's secret.

Lorenzo's story ends or begins at this point, depending upon how you look at it. As foster parents of the jaybird, our work was finished. The great, wild, free, wonderful Earth Mother had reclaimed what was hers all along. She has been in business longer than man's ancestors have been on this planet. Bungler that she sometimes is, she knows more about her affairs than we shall ever know.

Several years ago we closed the clinic and moved

away, but present owners tell us that Lorenzo and Loretta still defend that backyard as their own.

They also say that not one jaychick from many broods has ever fallen from the acacia tree.